# Burning Whispers

## A Jean Paul (JP) Kornig Novel

John F. Derr, RPh, FASCP, FHIMSS

The Reading Glass Books
1-888-420-3050
www.readingglassbooks.com
production@readingglassbooks.com

# Dedication

iii

To all Pharmacists

# Author's Note

"Dr. Hiroshi Nakasone is referenced in this work as a historical figure whose era and influence shaped postwar Japanese biomedical and industrial thinking; all scientific entities and events described are fictional."

# Author's Note on AI Use

This novel was written by the author, with selective assistance from artificial intelligence tools used for editing, research organization, and narrative clarity. These tools acted as a sounding board, not a creator. All ideas, characters, storylines, and final decisions remain entirely my own.

# Author's Note / Disclaimer

This is a work of fiction. Names, characters, organizations, governments, laws, and incidents are either the product of the author's imagination or are used fictitiously. Any resemblance to actual persons, living or dead, or to actual events or institutions is purely coincidental. Scientific descriptions, technologies, legal frameworks, and geopolitical references are imaginative constructions intended solely for storytelling. The author makes no claim regarding real programs, products, policies, or legislation of any nation or organization.

# Series Prologue: Venture Status Report

**Prepared by Founders:** Dr. Jean Paul (JP) Kornig, PharmD, FASCP, FHIMSS Amanda (Mandi) Kornig, MBA
**Location:** Anacortes, Washington
**Subject:** Summary of Completed Ventures and Corporate Realignment

**Completed Ventures**
    **Venture Study I — Ancient Cure: Deceptive Global Pharmaceutical Espionage Focus:** Development of LIFEAL™, an Alzheimer's therapy. **Source:** Alkaloids derived from *Alstonia scholaris* (Devil Tree; Dita; Milkwood Pine). **Outcome:** Breakthrough in plant-derived pharmaceuticals; exposed international espionage in drug development. Established ethnopharmacology as a credible research path.

    **Venture Study II — Rescued by Love™**
**Source:** Seneca Ranch **Focus:** Ethical implications of Premarin, a menopause therapy derived from pregnant mares' urine. **Outcome:** Publicized the hidden costs of pharmaceutical production; advanced advocacy for the humane treatment of draft horses.

    **Venture Study III — Whispers in the Grass™ Focus:** Introduction of Sweet Water Grass™, a cognitive-enhancing feed additive for equines. **Outcome:** Passage of U.S. federal legislation reclassifying horses as social animals rather than livestock, triggering cascading international policy alignment. Major slaughterhouses in Canada and Mexico were closed or converted to equine hospice facilities.

**Corporate Evolution**

James Pharmaceuticals →James–Bandai → JBD (James–Bandai–Danube)

**Bandai Integration:** Added DNA Bombardment research and manufacturing capacity. **Danube Partnership:** Expanded alkaloid research expertise; opened international distribution channels. **Challenge:** The "JBD" branding was cumbersome and lacked long-term vision.

Rebranding Initiative

**Objective:** Adopt a name of the major pharmaceutical company reflecting excellence and integrity. **Result:** Approval of the Greek word *aretē* (pronounced Ah-reh-TAY) as the new corporate identity. **Aretē Pharmaceutical™ (Ah-reh-TAY) Tagline:** Excellence in Science. Integrity in Care.

**Executive Summary:** Aretē Pharmaceutical™ is a global biopharmaceutical company reimagined from JBD. With operations across North America, Europe, and Asia, Aretē represents *aretē*—the pursuit of excellence—in the discovery, development, and delivery of medicines serving both humanity and animal health.

**Mission:** Transform inherited knowledge and modern science into safe, effective, and ethically developed medicines that enhance quality of life across generations. **Vision:** Build a future where innovation and integrity move together, with progress measured by the well-being of patients, animals, and communities.

**Current Position**

- Three Ventures completed and documented.
- Corporate identity stabilized under Aretē Pharmaceutical™.
- JP and Mandi Kornig now preparing a new strategic plan under their independent company, NinthWave Biobotanica.

## Author's Note to the Reader

This report closes one cycle and opens another. What began with Ancient Cure™, carried through the mares of Premarin, and matured with Sweet Water Grass™ has now set the foundation for a different kind of future. Mandi and I have stepped away from JBD—now reborn as Aretē Pharmaceutical™. Our path lies with NinthWave Biobotanica™, and the next Venture is about to begin.
— JP Kornig

# CHAPTER 1

## Anacortes, WA

"Are you ready, Mandi?" I asked, as we stood at the base of the trail climbing toward the top of Cap Sante, as the summer sky was just beginning to pale over Mount Baker. This was her first visit to the house I had bought on the hill. A place that would soon become our home, a location balanced between the working harbor of Anacortes and Cap Sante. At the time, the question felt simple, almost casual, the kind you ask when the future still looks like a view you're about to enjoy rather than a responsibility you're about to accept.

"Yep, JP. Let's go," she replied.

We took the stairs down to the main level of the house. Built into the side of Cap Sante peninsula—the peninsula overlooking Padilla Bay, not far from the oil refinery—the house had a clear view of Mount Baker from the deck. But this morning, we had decided to see the sunrise from the very top of Cap Sante.

We followed a hidden path leading upward. I wanted to show Mandi a place I had found where the tribes once watched canoe races on Guemes Channel, which separates Anacortes on Fidalgo Island from Guemes Island in Puget Sound.

The thick pine forest along the shore gave way to a large amphitheater-like clearing where long stone benches ran down the bank. It was a beautiful setting: channel waters at the bottom, forest framing the sides, and the rising sun beginning to light the space like stage lights in an open-air auditorium.

"JP, it's beautiful. Let's sit for a while. I can almost hear the crowd cheering on the racers. The silence makes it real."

After sitting quietly for a short period, we continued up the trail to the top of Cap Sante. There we found a parking area and large granite boulders on the east side that made natural seating for watching the sunrise.

Mount Baker loomed in the distance, about fifty miles from shore, its year-round snowcap glowing like a giant vanilla ice cream cone.

We sat on one of the rocks, facing east. Mount Baker, an active volcano, is part of the Pacific Ring of Fire, stretching from Asia through the Aleutians and down the U.S. Pacific coast.

The sun began to peek around the mountain, lighting its edges until it finally broke above the peak, outlining Mount Baker in gold.

"JP, I never knew Anacortes had views like this. You kept this from me," Mandi said, a playful spark in her eyes.

"It was meant as a surprise."

"Well, you succeeded. Most people think of the Northwest in terms of water and shoreline. But Mount Baker stands on its own."

We lingered until the sunrise fully unfolded, then began walking down the backside of Cap Sante, past the marina, and into town along Commercial Avenue.

"Where are we going?" Mandi asked.

"To Calico Cupboard," I said. "They're famous for their cinnamon rolls."

The bell over the door jingled as we stepped inside Calico Cupboard Café & Bakery, the air warm with the smell of fresh bread, cinnamon, and coffee. A glass case displayed sticky buns the size of fists and golden loaves cooling on racks.

"This place will ruin us," Mandi said with a smile.

We slid into a small table by the fogged window. The waitress poured steaming mugs of coffee before we even asked. I wrapped my hands around the cup, letting the heat sink in.

While we waited for plates of huevos rancheros and thick toast, I pulled a folded page from my pocket and laid it between us.

"What's this?" Mandi asked.

"Mandi, we've had many ventures over the last five years. Now we're an old married couple without a job—and far too young to retire. I thought we should spend the next few days figuring out what's next."

"I agree. It's time we act like grownups and get back to business." She tapped the paper. "So what's this?"

"You and I have vast experience in pharmaceuticals. I thought we could start with a list of questions. Not my plan, but our plan."

Mandi's eyes softened. "With all my heart. We make a great team—neither of us needs to command the other."

"Exactly. You bring product development and marketing. I bring research and business. Together, we're co-founders."

She leaned in. "Then here's the big question: what's the name of our company?"

I paused.

Mandi smiled. "You've always talked about the Ninth Wave—that rare wave of opportunity. I think this company is the NinthWave."

"Perfect," I said. "Now, what is the opportunity?"

Silence stretched between us before Mandi answered. "You are an ethnopharmacologist. How about plant-derived pharmaceuticals? That's always been our compass."

I nodded. "Then let's outline our questions."

**The Nine Questions of NinthWave Biobotanica™**
1. Who are we? *(identity, values, experience as individuals and as a team)*
2. What do we want to accomplish? *(core mission, desired impact)*
3. What are our assets? *(financial, technological, clinical, and experiential combined)*
4. What sets us apart? *(our edge—ethics, intelligence, partnerships)*
5. What opportunities exist in plant-derived pharmaceuticals? *(the future landscape)*
6. What is our Vision? *(long-term purpose)*
7. What is our Mission? *(practical mandate)*
8. What will success look like in 1, 5, and 10 years? *(growth and accountability)*
9. What is our Ninth Wave? *(our next Venture)*

Mandi leaned back, studying the page. "JP… do you realize something?"

"What's that?"

She turned the paper so I could see. "We started with ten questions. But look—once we grouped the assets together, we ended with nine."

I counted them slowly, then smiled. "Nine questions."

Mandi's eyes lit. "Nine waves. The last one—the crest beyond the others—is always the chance that changes everything."

I tapped the final line. "*What is our Ninth Wave?*

"That's the one we'll be chasing."

The waitress returned with warm cinnamon buns and more coffee. She smiled. "You two have been here over an hour. Are you writing a book?"

"Not exactly," Mandi said. "We're planning our future."

"Well, you look like a team. I bet you'll do fine."

We finished breakfast and walked back past the marina. Along the road, we passed old sea captains' homes with widow's walks, where wives once waited for their husbands' return from fishing voyages to Alaska and the Pacific.

By the time we reached home, the Great Room was filled with afternoon light. We spread our notes across the heavy log table—our new headquarters. By midnight, we had drafted the first ten pages of a business plan, giving shape and substance to the questions we had begun that morning.

Exhausted, we collapsed into bed with nothing more than a goodnight kiss.

Outside, the wind shifted across the bay—a quiet change in the air I didn't notice at the time.

Something new was already taking form, just beyond the edge of awareness.

# CHAPTER 2

# An Unexpected Letter

**Anacortes, WA**

We awoke refreshed after our long day of planning.

"JP, we've done a good job with our corporate planning," Mandi said. "But there's one question we haven't answered: what is our next venture?"

"You're right," I said. "We couldn't answer that until we had the business plan. For now, it's TBD—to be determined."

We reviewed the one-page summary aloud, line by line, making sure we were on the same page.

**NinthWave Biobotanica™ Business Plan Summary**

**"Secrets of the NinthWave — Where Global Intrigue Meets Plant Pharmaceuticals™"**

**Who We Are**
Veteran-founded and intelligence-driven, NinthWave Biobotanica transforms ancient ethnobotanical knowledge into modern pharmaceuticals. With AI-enhanced analysis and ethical sourcing, we develop plant-based medicines protected from espionage and built for global resilience.

**What Sets Us Apart**
- **Veteran leadership:** JP and Mandi Kornig blend scientific innovation with the operational discipline shaped by their military and pharmaceutical backgrounds.

- **Ethical discovery:** Indigenous partnerships and botanical archives ensure responsible benefit-sharing.
- **Intelligence advantage:** The TNIC™ (NinthWave Investigative Center) platform supports secure research and counterintelligence.
- **Strategic alliances:** Collaboration with Aretē Pharmaceutical strengthens scale and regulatory reach.

**Flagship Achievements**
- **LIFEAL™:** A breakthrough Alzheimer's therapy.
- **Premarin Alternatives:** Advancing humane pharmaceutical production.
- **Sweet Water Grass™:** Demonstrated equine cognition and contributed to horses being reclassified as social animals.

**Research Network**
- Big Timber. Montana — Alkaloid extraction and encapsulation
- Vienna, Austria — International development
- Bandai, Japan — DNA Bombardment and Advanced botanical delivery systems
- New York City — Legacy research archives
- Mammoth Lakes, California — TNIC AI hub

**Strategic Vision**
Develop safe, effective plant-derived pharmaceuticals—and protect them from global interference. NinthWave aims to unite science, intelligence, and ethics in a way that strengthens patient care and national resilience.

**Tagline**
Innovation with Integrity. Intelligence with Purpose.

The doorbell startled us.

I checked my phone's camera door feed: a Navy Lieutenant in khakis stood outside, holding a sealed leather pouch.

"Good morning, sir," he said when I opened the door. "I have documents requiring your signature. Strict instructions—hand delivery only."

Puzzled, I signed and accepted the envelope. Inside was another, sealed with heavy tape. Across it, bold letters read:

**TOP SECRET/NOFORN — FOR YOUR EYES ONLY**

Mandi leaned over my shoulder, exhaling sharply. "JP… this looks serious. Are you being brought back into Active Duty?"

I gave a half-smile. "I don't know. But as a former Secret Control Officer, I know what these words mean. I have to read this memo alone."

I stepped out onto the deck to read the letter in private.

**TOP SECRET/NOFORN
FOR YOUR EYES ONLY**

**THE PENTAGON
WASHINGTON, D.C.
DEPARTMENT OF DEFENSE**
Office of the Assistant Secretary of Defense for Health Affairs

**PERSONAL COVER MEMORANDUM**
From: Vice Admiral Albert Brewer, M.D.
Assistant Secretary of Defense for Health Affairs
(U.S. Navy, Retired)

To: Capt. J. P. Kornig, USN (Ret.)

Subj: Invitation to Closed Briefing — Combat Deep Burn Therapy & Force Readiness Ref: (A) Prior staff service, Atlantic Task Force — USS *Dewey* (DLG-14)

It has been too long since our wardroom days. I read with real pleasure of your recent marriage—please extend my congratulations to Mandi.

I am writing under personal cover, though in my official capacity, regarding a matter of urgency affecting combat medicine and force rotation.

In forward theaters, troop rotation is increasingly constrained by missile burn injuries for which current therapies are inadequate. My research director and I have assessed that your background in ethnopharmacology, coupled with Mandi's pharmaceutical strategy expertise, may align with a path we have not yet explored.

You are invited to a TOP SECRET briefing at the Pentagon with:
    a. The undersigned;
    b. A Marine Medical Corps General; and
    c. My senior burn research lead.

**Objective:** Determine whether your expertise can be directed into a classified program with potential for a government research contract.

For scheduling and clearances, contact my office on the secure line below. Mandi may participate in planning discussions; but this initial meeting will be limited to the four of us.

**Handling:** This memorandum is FOR YOUR EYES ONLY. Do not duplicate. Do not discuss by unsecured means. Return or destroy per instructions after use. NOTE: You can share with Mandi.

Respectfully,
Albert Brewer, M.D.
Assistant Secretary of Defense for Health Affairs
(Vice Admiral, Medical Corps, U.S. Navy, Retired)
Secure Line: (202) 555-1212
Copy: 1 of 1 • Control No.: TS-BW-2025-001

I rocked back and forth in my deck chair and thought about Admiral Brewer's letter. This was perfect timing for a new venture—for Mandi, for me, and for NinthWave Biobotanica. We were looking for a project, and one had just dropped into our laps. But did we want to get tied up in a government venture?

After spending time at the Pentagon during my Active Naval Reserve years, I knew Washington could be tiresome and staff-heavy. Yet Admiral

Brewer was a trusted friend, and I was sure he would not mislead me. I had to agree with him If he thought Mandi and I could break his research deadlock. He knew what he wanted to accomplish, and he knew me. We would not be working with strangers.

The alternative was to start from scratch in hunting for our first project as NinthWave Biobotanica. To use a very old saying: don't look a gift horse in the mouth.

I tucked the letter into my pants pocket and walked back into the Great Room, which had become our makeshift office.

Mandi was just setting down the phone.

"Who was the call from?" I asked.

"Remember that young woman you introduced me to the first day I visited you up here in Anacortes?"

"Sure. Her name was Shana Lawrence, and her dad was the lead contractor on this house. Shana did the interior decorating." I paused. "That Shana?"

"Yes. She wanted to welcome us home and asked if she could come over and discuss something about her grandfather."

I raised my eyebrows. Shana mentioning her grandfather—after our months earlier conversation with him about firework burns—felt less like coincidence and more like a pattern demanding attention.

"What is that look on your face?" Mandi asked.

"Forgive me—we just tripped over three signals at once."

"The letter?"

"Yes. Let's go onto the deck."

We sat in the rockers. I took a deep breath. "In the last thirty minutes:"

"One—we finished the Nine Questions; the last was 'What's our next venture?'"

"Two—Admiral Brewer sends a For-Your-Eyes-Only letter asking for our help."

"Three—Shana calls about a burn-care solution from her grandfather."

"That's not noise, Mandi."

She watched me closely. "That is… incredulous."

We'd encountered chance before, but never in a stack like this.

"What do we do?" she asked.

"Invite Shana to dinner. If she mentions her grandfather, have him come." I hesitated. "And Admiral Brewer wants me in D.C. for a small, high-level meeting. I plan to accept."

Mandi said nothing. We had promised to work together, but this time the first step would be mine.

"Mandi," I said, pulling the letter from my pocket, "I want you to read Admiral Brewer's letter, and then we'll discuss the label: *FOR YOUR EYES ONLY.*"

She read the letter twice. As I had done, she leaned back in her rocking chair and thought for a few minutes.

I followed up. "You'll note that Admiral Brewer said you and I can discuss this venture together, as well as work jointly in the planning stage should we accept it. My intuition is that I will go to the Pentagon for the meeting, and then, when I return, we'll discuss the project. It also means that for now, you and I are the only ones who can talk about this opportunity. It's TOP SECRET/NOFORN—no foreign access."

I paused.

"Is this okay with you?"

"I can't say I like not being involved up front," she said, "but I do understand."

The phone started to ring.

"I'll get it," Mandi said.

She answered. "It's Shana, and she wants to talk to you."

"Shana, I understand you'd like to get together," I said. "Great—why don't you join Mandi and me for dinner tonight, say 6:30 PM?" I paused. "Fine, see you then." Another pause. "If you'd like your grandfather to join you, that would be fine, Shana. We look forward to seeing both of you at 6:30." I hung up the phone.

I looked at Mandi. "Well, we're starting the ball rolling toward our next venture. I'll call Admiral Brewer's assistant and set up my meeting at the Pentagon."

I picked up the phone and dialed **202-555-1212**.

# Chapter 3

# Dinner and Trip Planning

**Anacortes House**

"Mandi, let's adjourn to the deck and think about next steps. But first, let's crack a bottle of what would become our favorite Chuckanut wine—Baylight Cellars Pinot Noir—and have a celebration drink to our possible next venture and happy coincidences."

As Mandi stepped out onto the deck, I swung by the kitchen and picked up one of the many bottles of Pinot Noir along with a couple of glasses.

It was early afternoon, the kind where time feels suspended. The sun hung high but had begun its slow descent toward the western horizon.

"A toast—to us, to Biobotanica, and to our first possible venture as a husband-and-wife team."

We clicked glasses, settled into our chairs, and watched the light shift across the slopes of Mount Baker.

After a few minutes of quiet celebration and reflection, Mandi asked, "What will Shana and her grandfather want to talk about?"

"Her grandfather's English name is Danny Whulshad. He and his brother are members of the Whulshad tribe, an ancient people with deep roots in this region. Danny actually made the rocking chairs we're sitting in. He's both a chemist and a craftsman—and the person who first got me interested in coming up to Anacortes from Westwood Village, CA.

"He wanted me to look at a salve he'd developed from a tree grown near the edge of the Olympic Peninsula, close to the national park. He believed it could be an effective treatment for burns caused by fireworks. At the time, I did only a cursory market analysis and concluded that the consumer market wouldn't support the development costs. I turned him down."

I took another sip of wine before continuing. "Now that we have a letter pointing toward a potential government burn contract, I think we should take another look. But we shouldn't raise the topic ourselves. Let Shana or Danny bring it up."

I added, "This will be our first test in secrecy. There should be no mention of my up coming meeting or the Admiral's letter."

Mandi nodded. "I have a suggestion on strategy. Until we understand what the Pentagon offer is really about, we should learn everything we can about the current burn-treatment market—the competitors, the products, the features and benefits."

She continued, "Admiral Brewer is approaching this from a military perspective. Since we don't yet know the specifics, let's assume it intersects with existing burn therapies. If you go into the Pentagon meeting already fluent in the domestic and international burn-treatment landscape, you'll be positioned as an expert from the start."

I smiled. "I knew there was more than love that made me want you as my business partner. You're absolutely right."

We toasted again.

The shadows lengthened as the afternoon eased toward evening. After a few more glasses of Pinot Noir, I checked the time.

"Mandi, it's 5:30 PM. They'll be here in an hour."

She jumped up. "It's too late to cook. We need privacy, so let's eat in."

"I was thinking the same thing, Dungeness crab and salmon, sides, dessert. Your herbal iced tea, And I have huckleberry tea from Montana. It'll make good conversation."

"Perfect."

We cleared the Great Room table and prepared for our guests. The first knock was Anthony's with the food. The second, right on time at 6:30, was Shana and her grandfather.

We served the meal family-style. When I poured the huckleberry tea into small glasses, its deep red color caught Shana's eye.

"Huckleberry?" she asked. "I've never tried that."

"It's from Montana," I said. "A little tart, a little sweet."

Danny lifted his glass, inhaled, then took a sip. "Unique," he said. "It reminds me that medicine doesn't always live in laboratories. Sometimes it lives in the land."

Mandi met my eyes and gave a small nod.

Dinner unfolded easily—talk of Anacortes, the house Shana's father built, and local history.

Dessert had just been served when Shana shifted the conversation.

"JP," she said carefully, "there's something we discussed on your first visit to Anacortes that I'd like to bring up again. I want Mandi to understand my grandfather's work beyond furniture. Do we have time?"

"Of course," Mandi said.

Shana leaned forward. "Before your venture into *Whispers in the Grass,* you and I talked about my grandfather's burn salve originally developed for fireworks. Do you remember?"

"I do," I said. "We met in his lab." The lab was near La Conner, across the channel that separates Fidalgo Island from the mainland. "He showed me the salve and demonstrated its effects on pig skin that had been obtained humanely and with permission."

"Yes," Shana said. "You told us the market wouldn't support the development costs of a fireworks salve."

"That was my conclusion at the time."

Danny had been quiet, listening. Finally, he spoke. "Shana, let me continue."

He explained his path. "After Purdue University, where I earned a degree in chemical engineering with a thesis on burns, I went to work at a large corporate burn-therapy lab. Eventually, I came back home. During my corporate years, I worked with hyperbaric oxygen chambers. They were effective, but impractical. Expensive, and useless in the field outside institutional settings."

He paused. "So I came back home. Back to La Conner, where I built a small lab over my uncle's old workshop. It's not corporate, but it works for me. After your rejection, I shifted my focus from fireworks burns to kitchen burns—deeper, lingering injuries that affect family livelihoods."

"I thought, if I could bridge the gap between aloe and surgery, between folk remedy and hospital care, there would be a market. Maybe not a corporate market, but one that matters."

Silence settled over the deck.

I realized how wrong my earlier assumptions had been not about his science, but about the man and his story.

Shana broke the silence. "Grandfather, you never told me this. I'm so proud of you."

Danny lowered his head slightly. "I apologize."

"You don't need to," I said. "You should be proud."

Mandi nodded. "And we hope somehow we can find a way to work together."

I added, "Danny, for your information we've formed a new company here in Anacortes—NinthWave Biobotanica. I have one question. Did you do all of this alone?"

He hesitated. "I have a partner—my brother, Caleb Whulshad. He's the licensed curator of a Pacific Yew plantation near Olympic National Park, outside Sequim."

Danny explained Caleb's work supplying bark for cancer drugs, and how synthetic substitutes had collapsed the market and how Danny had began experimenting with discarded bark scraps.

Danny in a hopeful voice said, "Perhaps since you are now working in Anacortes, you can find other uses for the Pacific Yew,"

Not yet disclosing to Danny the potential work on burn salves, Mandi commented, "That is interesting." and asked, "How would we get to Sequim?"

"JP, I understand that you have a Nordic Tug?" Danny said. "You can take it across Puget Sound and the Strait of Juan de Fuca. Sequim is on the shore of the Olympic Peninsula. You can tie up at John Wayne Marina."

Shana smiled. "Yes, that John Wayne."

Danny continued, "Call Caleb when you're coming. Be prepared to hike—and to stay overnight."

I said, "I have a Pentagon meeting in Washington, D.C., next week," I paused. "Mandi can make the trip to Sequim while I am in DC."

We agreed.

Later, Mandi and Shana talked logistics while Danny and I shared Purdue stories. He had graduated five years before me. To orient him to NinthWave I gave him our one-page summary of the Business Plan.

When Danny and Shana left, the house felt charged with possibility.

"What do you think?" I asked.

Mandi smiled. "I think we should grab our robes, another bottle of Pinot Noir, and end this perfect evening with a trip to our deck jacuzzi."

Above us, stars broke through the evening clouds. After a night of coincidences and guarded truths, it felt right to end with something simple. Just warmth, quiet, and the promise of what might come next.

# CHAPTER 4

# Planning Paths

**Scene One: Anacortes House — Thursday Morning**

The next morning, Mandi and I woke earlier than usual. Yesterday's coincidences still buzzed as fragments in our brains. Now it was time to pull everything together. We agreed to run on two travel investigated tracks until the end of the week.

Another warm fall day settled over Anacortes. Nervous energy carried us through breakfast until the reality of preparing for two separate trips—mine to Washington, D.C., and Mandi's to Sequim to meet with Caleb—finally developed.

When we stepped into the Great Room, the mess from the day before hit us. What should have been the heart of NinthWave Biobotanica™ looked instead like a storage yard—maps, laptops, notebooks, and scattered files spread across the long table. The fireplace sat unused. Outside, the windows framed Padilla Bay, calm and bright, while inside the space felt improvised and temporary.

When Shana's father, Jim (the contractor and builder of the house) stopped by to check on things, I caught him before he left.

"Jim, before you go, could you help us rethink the Great Room? NinthWave isn't a kitchen-table operation anymore. We need the Great Room to function as both as an office and a living area. A place for strategy and a place for life."

Jim surveyed the clutter and nodded thoughtfully. "Built-in shelving, a privacy partition, better lighting. We'll keep the comfort but give you a functioning headquarters."

"Exactly," I said. "We're moving fast. This room needs to keep up."

**Scene Two: Thursday Midday**

Shortly after noon, Shana joined Mandi and I as she was familiar with Sequim. Within minutes, she and Mandi were leaning over a nautical map of the Strait of Juan de Fuca, marking the route the Nordic Tug would take to Sequim.

"If we leave Monday morning, the Nordic Tug will get us to John Wayne Marina by early afternoon," Mandi said.

Mandi thought that it would be helpful if they added another member to the group. She had kept in close contact with her sister, Mariah Haynes, at Seneca Ranch, Big Timber, Montana since their development of Sweet Water Grass™ horse feed additive.

Together, Mandi and I had advised Mariah and the ranch's research director, Penilia, on building a dedicated alkaloid research laboratory. When it came time for Mariah to staff the new research facility, they brought in one of the best: Dr. Cam Williamson.

Cam was more than another lab hand. With deep training in pharmacognosy, he had become a rising authority on alkaloid chemistry— the art of isolating and refining plant compounds capable of healing or harming with equal precision. His work bridged traditional knowledge and modern discovery, and we had long viewed him as a future recruit.

Because NinthWave staffing goals was to keep staffing lean, Cam was the natural choice for NinthWave to subcontract Seneca Ranch for alkaloid research projects.

Mandi also knew about Cam's brother, Chris Williamson, who lived in Seattle. A respected field phytochemist, Chris was the kind of scientist who could move seamlessly from forest to laboratory. Exactly the skill set needed for the Sequim trip.

Mandi briefed me on adding Chris to the team. I agreed immediately.

She called Cam for Chris's contact information. Cam readily shared it. Cam had already briefed Chris on the Alkaloid lab and Chris was enthusiastic about working with his brother. When Mandi called Chris, he offered to drive up to Anacortes the next morning.

**Scene Three: Thursday Afternoon**

I turned back to my own work.

"Mandi, I need The NinthWave Investigative Center (TNIC™) involved."

"What will you be asking for?"

"A full analysis of the burn-treatment market, domestic and international. Every product, every competitor, every weakness, every opportunity. I want it by Saturday so I can build my Pentagon briefing."

Mandi rested a hand on my shoulder. "Maybe you should give the task directly to Skip Howard, the Director of TNIC, and then fly to Mammoth Lakes on Saturday morning. You made Skip a partner in NinthWave, but he doesn't know yet what we're working on."

She continued, "If you stay at the Mammoth Lakes TNIC house, you and Skip can work on the Pentagon PowerPoint together, and have dinner at Anne's Grill before you fly on to San Francisco and connect commercially to a plane to Washington, D.C. When you return from your meeting next Thursday to pick up your plane, you can brief Skip on anything new from the Pentagon."

I stared at her, impressed. "Mandi, you are a genius. That's a perfect plan."

I tapped a secure TNIC line. Within minutes of discussion, Skip confirmed the agenda and was energized to help NinthWave's newest direction.

Two paths were forming. One across the water to Sequim, and one across the country to Washington, D.C., by way of Mammoth Lakes.

## Scene Four: Friday Morning

Chris arrived early, from Seattle where he had an apartment. He was tall and broad-shouldered, with the easy stride of someone who has spent more time outdoors than indoors. He shook Mandi's and my hand firmly.

"Great to meet you, Chris," Mandi said warmly. "If you're anything like your brother Cam, we'll have a successful venture to Sequim."

She added, "Chris, I want you to meet Shana Lawrence. She'll be working with us on the fact-gathering trip to Sequim and the Pacific Yew plantation on Monday."

Chris and Shana bumped fists, and there was a spark of recognition.

"Do you two know each other?" Mandi asked.

Together, perfectly in sync, they said, "We both attended the University of Washington."

Then, turning toward each other, they silently mouthed, *Go Dawgs.*

Mandi laughed. "I can see getting you two acquainted won't be a problem. Chris, I'll let Shana brief you on the mission."

Chris smiled. "That's fine by me."

While the three of them reviewed maps, the gear they would require, and Danny's specific instructions for the trip, I moved to the far end of the table with my own work.

The TNIC burn packet was taking shape—silver sulfadiazine, aloe derivatives, stem-cell grafting techniques, hyperbaric chamber statistics. Products, patents, price points, failure modes. I outlined what my Pentagon briefing needed to address: the gaps, the opportunities, the current dead ends.

I emailed the outline to Skip.

## Scene Five: Friday Evening

By sundown, both travel groups had momentum.

Shana, Chris, and Mandi finalized supplies for the Sequim trip—sleeping bags, trail gear, herbal tea. Chris checked items off the list with the calm certainty of someone who had walked those woods many times.

On my side of the room, I had sent Skip the full outline of tasks for Saturday. I gathered my notes and the research I had compiled on burn treatments, sliding everything into a folder. I had a backup hard copy just incase the email did not go through.

When Shana and Chris left, the house quieted. Mandi and I stepped onto the deck and eased into our rocking chairs, satisfied with what we had achieved in just three days.

Mandi poured two glasses of wine. "Two paths," she said softly, raising her glass. "Sequim and D.C. Both starting next week!"

We clinked glasses.

Behind us, the Great Room was still half-office, half-home—but it was already becoming the headquarters of something larger.

The last sunlight on Mount Baker faded into the Pacific.

# CHAPTER 5

# TNIC and the Pentagon Plan

**Scene One: Flight to Mammoth Lakes, CA**

The alarm went off at 4:30 AM. I moved quietly through the house, careful not to wake Mandi. By 5:00 AM I was out on the deck, the predawn air sharp against my face. Below, in the hangar tucked under the deck, the Cessna Caravan Amphibian waited—gleaming silver-gray in the dim light.

At 5:15 AM I pushed the hangar door button and they rumbled open beneath the deck. I engaged the engine and eased the Caravan out of its berth. The floats slipped silently into Padilla Bay.

Beside Caravan, the Nordic Tug rested in its slip, rocking gently as if in farewell.

Inside the cockpit, the instrument panel glowed to life. I ran the preflight checks with the ease of muscle memory—fuel clean, hydraulics steady, flaps set. On the radio, clearance came crisp from Naval Air Station Whidbey Island, which controlled the airspace around Anacortes. They still had my name in their flight records. The air controller gave a clipped military "cleared for departure." It was a familiarity I hadn't felt in years.

I throttled forward. The Caravan gathered speed, carving a silver wake across the flat water.

Spray fanned wide as the floats skimmed faster, until, with a smooth lift of the nose, the plane broke free. Padilla Bay dropped away beneath me, the shoreline lights shrinking to sparks in the predawn dark.

### *Climb and Cruise*
I headed south, keeping the Cascades to port and Seattle and then Portland to starboard.

I retracted the floats into the wheel configuration, ready for the pavement landings ahead. By the time I cleared the Cascades, the eastern sky was on fire. Mount Rainier's snowcap glowed first, then Mount Hood, then the perfect blue ring of Crater Lake.

The Caravan settled into cruise at 10,000 feet, 185 knots. To the east, dawn spread across the mountains. To the west the sun's rays were easing across the Pacific, the coastline tracing a thin line of silver.

At 8:30 AM, Mount Shasta rose out of the haze like a stone titan. I banked slightly west, nose angling toward Redding, CA.

### *Fuel Stop — Redding Municipal (KRDD)*
Touchdown came easy on Redding's long runway. The amphibious floats rode steady in their storage bay as the wheels took the weight. I taxied in and while refueling stretched my stiff legs. Meanwhile, the Caravan drank its fill of aviation gas.

The terminal coffee was bitter as it was probably made by an ex-Navy pilot. It seemed like every pot of coffee made by a Navy man had been strained through cigarette butts and kept in a metal coffee pot simmering for hours. There was no definition for Navy coffee taste. But one thing you count on, it was hot.

I checked the weather—clear skies ahead, with light Sierra turbulence expected on descent into Mammoth Lakes, CA.

By 9:15 AM I was airborne again, climbing east toward Reno.

### Crossing the Sierra Nevada

The ridge lines sharpened as I pushed into the Sierra Nevada Mountains. Jagged granite, glacial lakes flashing blue, and dark forests unspooled below. Beyond the final ridge, Mono Lake shimmered like a sheet of hammered silver.

I began my descent into Mammoth Lakes, aware of the thin air tugging at the Caravan's wings.

### Landing — Mammoth Yosemite Airport (KMMH)

Mammoth sits at more than seven thousand feet above sea level—an altitude that punishes mistakes. Aircraft instruments are usually calibrated for sea level, and if a pilot doesn't account for density altitude and recalibrate for a higher altitude when landing at Mammoth Yosemite Airport your plane will dig a hole. Landing errors here are not forgiving.

I extended the wheel landing gear, listening for the familiar hydraulic whine as the wheels locked into place.

"Gear down and a green board." I confirmed.

The final approach had been tight, downdrafts nudging at the wings. I corrected with small, deliberate inputs, riding the Caravan steadily onto the runway like I had always done over the many years of skiing Mammoth Mountain. The wheels kissed pavement, the floats balanced clean in their storage, and the plane rolled out smooth.

### Arrival — Mammoth Lakes, CA

On the apron, a dark SUV idled near the tarmac. Marine Corps Colonel Skip Howard (Ret.) stood beside it, hands in his jacket pockets, watching the Caravan taxi in. His posture hadn't changed, steady, unreadable, and a trace of a smile surfaced when I swung the hatch open.

I shut down the engine, climbed down from the float step, and crossed the warm Sierra asphalt.

"Skip," I said, extending my hand.

"Welcome to Mammoth Lakes," he replied, gripping my hand firmly followed by a bear hug and mutual slaps on backs, "We've got a lot to talk about!"

The mountains towered above us, crisp against the noon sky, as I followed my old friend toward the SUV and the hidden heart of TNIC.

**Scene Two: The Ninth Wave Investigative Center (TNIC™)**

Skip drove easily from the airport, crossed Highway 395, and turned into downtown Mammoth Lakes.

He headed toward what had once been my ski home at 13 Snow Run Drive, before I married Mandi ending my bachelor life and moving to our primary home to Anacortes.

The house sat on a wooded corner lot, two blocks from the Mammoth Mountain ski lifts. Three bedrooms occupied the lower level, while a large Great Room spanned the second floor to capture the view. Glass walls and redwood decks wrapped three sides of the upper level, positioned to maximize sun and showcase the Sierra slopes.

I had lived here nearly year-round. Once I decided to move to Anacortes, Skip and I decided to relocate TNIC from Westwood Village near UCLA to Mammoth Lakes.

When we were working from our Westwood Apartment, artificial intelligence was still in its infancy. Our computer system—AIMS™— had been cutting-edge for its time. It was instrumental in projects like Ancient Cure's Venture, LIFEAL™, but it no longer met the demands of a modern healthcare intelligence platform. The remodeled TNIC transformed the house into something years ahead of most of the big AI contractors. We moved into the Quantum era when we developed the Q'ARIUM computer system.

Now TNIC served as both an AI center and a home for Skip and Annie, with a separate guest wing for visiting experts. Mandi and I had helped design the guest quarters.

The Q'ARIUM Computer system served as the cutting-edge quantum backbone for the Quantum Whisper Bridge (QWB), blending real-world quantum principles with advanced cybersecurity engineering to enable ultra-secure, emission-free data capture.

At its core are arrays of superconducting qubits. Tiny circuits chilled to near-absolute zero in cryogenic chambers housed in the TNIC basement servers, which harness quantum superposition and entanglement to process information in ways classical computers can't, like instantly detecting and recording subtle "variances" in quantum states without sending any signals.

Power came from efficient solar panels on the roof, supplemented by redundant batteries to maintain the delicate quantum environment, while integrated classical AI modules (evolved from the older AIMS™ system) handled error correction and interfaces with users.

In operation, the Q'ARIUM "listens" passively to quantum fluctuations, storing them in tamper-proof vials or patches that self-destruct, erasing the data forever, if accessed by anyone but the intended recipient, ensuring secrets remain whispers lost to the void upon any unauthorized glance. This Quantum set up would assist us in setting up a communication link between members of the security cleared team. The Quantum Whisper Bridge (QWB) would be our secure communication method, but right now Skip and I had to catch up on our rapid moving lives.

"Annie is still running her café," Skip said when I asked about Skip's wife Annie. "We'll see her tonight."

We spent the next few minutes reminiscing about the past life in the military and running AIMS in Westlake Village.

Skip stopped our reminiscing by bringing us back to the purpose of the visit. "JP, we've got real work ahead of us if you're attending a Pentagon meeting next week." He paused to see my reaction which was a little disconcerting after being cut off.

Skip knew me and he paused so I could get back on the subject of the Pentagon meeting. He continued: "I read your email last night and I pulled together what we'll need to do today from your task list."

"Who did you bring in as a subject matter expert (SME) to assist us?" I asked.

"A consumer expert on the burn-care market. You probably remember her—she was the Navy pharmacist corpsman on the USS Dewey with you. Since leaving the Navy, she has worked her way up into dermatologic product leadership."

"That sounds perfect," I said.

"Good. But first," Skip added, "since I don't know what you and Mandi have been building since you got married, let's adjourn to the deck for lunch. You can brief me on NinthWave Biobotanica and this new venture."

"Fair enough."

Skip said, "Give me a minute and I will join you on the deck."

"No problem, I want to look at the mountain and relive my time when I was young and an expert skier." I walked out onto the deck which faced the mountain and the 11,053 feet above sea level peak of Mammoth Mountain. The peak had a deep snow over hang. The ski run off the peak was named Climax and was an extremely sharp drop off before making the run down to the Chair lift that would take the skier back to the top. If you started at the base lodge, you could reach the peak by gondola.

Mammoth Mountain Ski Area, CA

### Flashback

As I stood on the deck and looked up at the Cornice, my mind drifted back years to my first run down that magnificent, packed-powder slope. It was a sunny day, as most Mammoth days were. I stood at the top, looking almost straight down an almost vertical drop. I traversed the peak with my left shoulder brushing the side of the mountain, staring down as I worked up the nerve to turn right and commit.

That was the first challenge. The second was staying upright while holding an angle that matched the pitch of the slope. The third was controlling my speed—keeping it reasonable without losing my edge, which would have meant crashing and tumbling down the rest of Climax.

The run fell away for nearly a thousand vertical feet, and if you skied it clean, you made the descent in under a minute—long enough to make you question every decision that brought you to the edge.

After that inaugural run, I skied it once every year, just to prove I still had the nerve. As I grew older and the thought of falling and rolling down the slope began to dominate my mind, I decided I had nothing left to prove. I had made the run clean. I stopped.

Over the years, I often thought about designing a T-shirt celebrating the ultimate Climax. Since Mammoth Mountain is classified as a dormant volcano—capable of erupting at any time—the design seemed obvious. A skier racing down Climax, lava licking at the backs of his skis, snow spraying ahead as the skier outran the volcano. Above the image, the words:

**THE ULTIMATE CLIMAX**

The Mammoth Lakes Chamber of Commerce didn't appreciate people talking about dormant volcanoes—they worried it would scare skiers away. But like many towns living under volcanic threat, the experience outweighed the risk.

**Scene Three: The International Burn Market**
Skip interrupted my thoughts when he and his subject matter expert came onto the deck for lunch. Skip introduced Karen Mitchell Lieutenant Colonel, USMC (Ret.). She moved with the controlled precision of someone who had lived under orders for decades.

Karen laid out the burn-treatment landscape with clinical clarity: legacy silver creams that scar, consumer botanicals plagued by unstable supply chains, European hydrogels too costly and fragile for combat, and advanced therapies impressive on paper but impossible to deploy forward.

"The problem," she concluded, "isn't demand. It's penetration. Every topical solution fails where it matters most."

Her analysis framed my Pentagon briefing exactly as I needed it, showing knowledge without revealing intent.

# CHAPTER 6

# Security and Q'ARIUM

**Scene one: Q'ARIUM**

After Karen left, Skip gathered the empty cups and nodded toward the stairwell leading to the basement.

"You should see what you, our computer buddy Peter Peterson ($P^2$) and I built," Skip said.

The hum reached us before we hit the bottom step—low, steady, almost alive. The Q'ARIUM core occupied the reinforced lower level, not crowded, not flashy. The layout felt deliberate, as if the system needed room to think.

"Hard to believe this replaced AIMS," I said.

Our buddy, $P^2$ stood near the primary console, hands relaxed at his sides, watching the data the way a pilot watches weather. We exchanged pleasantries and $P^2$ launched into his favorite subject the Q'ARIUM.

"AIMS was linear," he said. "Fast. Powerful. But it chased answers along predefined paths."

"And Q'ARIUM?" I asked.

"It explores states," Skip said. "Probability before certainty."

Streams of data branched, collapsed, and recombined, less like computation, more like consideration.

"This is what changed everything," I said quietly.

P² nodded. "Q'ARIUM doesn't look for people. It looks for improbable coordination. When something crosses a threshold, it can't hide."

"Even if you don't yet know how to explain it," Skip added.

I understood the implication immediately. Raw intelligence was one thing. Making it comprehensible was another.

"When we built this," Skip said, "we weren't thinking about the Pentagon."

"No," I replied. "We were thinking about truth."

"And now," he said, "truth has consequences."

Back upstairs, the mood shifted.

"If the Pentagon moves forward," I said, "they'll want more than analysis. They'll want communication—secure, silent, global."

P² leaned against the counter, considering.

"That's a different problem," he said.

"Which is why I'm calling it the Quantum Whisper Bridge (QWB)," I replied. "It's not a system yet. It's a requirement."

P² looked at me for a long moment.

"Q'ARIUM can think in whispers," he said slowly. "But it still speaks in signals."

"That gap matters," I said. "If it behaves like conventional systems, it's already compromised."

P² allowed himself the slightest smile.

"We can build QWB as part of the Q'ARIUM system," P² said. "But it won't look like anything they expect."

"It shouldn't," I replied.

He nodded once. "Then we're aligned."

Skip exhaled, satisfied. "I told you. You'd forget what AIMS ever felt like."

I was already there.

## Scene Two: Annie's Bar & Grill — Saturday Evening

That night, Skip and I drove into town as the sun dropped behind the Sierra crest. The temperature fell fast, the way it always did in Mammoth once daylight faded. Lights flickered on along Main Street, reflecting off patches of old snow pushed against the curbs.

We passed the dark shell of Whiskey Creek, its sign unlit. A quiet reminder of how quickly things could change. Mammoth endured, but never casually.

Annie's Bar & Grill glowed ahead, warm light spilling onto the sidewalk. Skis were stacked by the door despite the late hour. A snowcat rumbled past on its way toward the mountain, beginning another night's work.

Inside, the dinner rush was thinning. The late crowd of lift operators and ski patrol were finishing their meals, parkas half-zipped, boots unlaced. A ski patrolman settled his tab at the bar, helmet tucked under his arm, with a folded up trail map and herding a tired group of non drinking teen agers toward the door.

Annie moved among the group easily, part host, part guardian. She refilled water glasses, exchanged a few last words, thanked people by name. One by one, coats went on, chairs slid back, and the room slowly emptied.

When the final customer stepped out into the cold, Annie flipped the sign on the door to *Closed* and turned the lock. The sound was small but decisive.

Only then did she look at us and smile.

"Now," she said, "I can actually sit down." Annie looked over at me. Years ago before Skip, we had been an item. Once she had met Skip, there was no one else in her world.

She poured herself a cup of coffee, wiped her hands on a towel out of habit more than need, and slid into the booth across from us. The grill was quiet now, the kitchen lights dimmed, the warmth lingering in the air.

"Don't tell me you've had him locked up all day," she said, nodding toward me.

"Only for the good of the Republic," Skip replied.

She snorted softly. "The Republic can wait. You look like you need food."

She disappeared briefly into the kitchen and returned with stew and lake trout, already plated.

Outside the window, Mammoth Mountain loomed dark and patient, its upper runs swallowed by night.

"This town runs on people who know how to wait," Annie said as she set the plates down.

"Weather, snow, tourists. You learn patience here or you leave."

As we ate, I gave her the short version, no acronyms, no details that didn't belong outside this table. Just the idea. Burns. Treatment. A chance to do something useful.

She listened carefully, eyes steady.

"Burns," she said after a moment. "They don't care who you are or what you planned to do with your life."

"No," I agreed.

She glanced toward the locked door, then back to us. "This place survives because people look out for each other. On the mountain. In town. When someone goes down, everyone notices."

Her gaze settled on me.

"When you are working at the Pentagon, don't forget the people behind the acronyms."

The words landed clean and solid.

We lingered in the quiet that followed. No clatter of dishes now. No voices. Just the low hum of refrigeration and the faint sound of wind outside, moving through the trees.

For a while, it wasn't about TNIC or the Pentagon. It was about trust of the past and future. Choices that would travel far beyond Annie's Bar and Grill and this small mountain town.

# CHAPTER 7

# Visit to the Pacific Yew Plantation

### Olympic Peninsula, Washington

**Scene One: Saturday Afternoon — Sequim Trip Planning**

Mandi called a trip-preparation meeting for Saturday afternoon with Shana and Chris. Charts and maps were spread across the Great Room table as they talked through the route to Sequim and John Wayne Marina, where they would meet Caleb Whulshad. They also listed what they would need for their visit to the yew grove.

Shana was a great help; she had been to the Pacific Yew grove many times, assisting her grandfather in gathering raw materials for his topical burn salve.

Mandi laid out a rough plan so they could make sure they had enough supplies.

**Sunday**
5:00 AM – 12:00 PM — **Take the Nordic Tug to Sequim. Estimated six to seven hours, depending on sea state.**
12:00 – 1:00 PM — Meet Caleb for lunch and an introduction to the Pacific Yew.
1:00 – 2:00 PM — Drive to trailhead (specific location to be provided by Caleb).
2:00 – 4:00 PM — Hike to cabin and grove.
Evening — Dinner and discussion about the yew. Bunk in Caleb's cabin.

**Monday** — Full day at the yew grove, learning more about the tree and raw-material harvesting for cancer pharmaceuticals.

**Tuesday** — Depart mid-morning, returning home by Nordic Tug before supper.

"What do you guys think about this schedule?" Mandi asked.

Shana nodded. "It's general, but it works. I've been to the grove many times after graduation, helping my grandfather. We usually take the ferry to Port Townsend and drive to the trailhead. I do advise warm clothing and bedding as it gets cold at night, at roughly thirty-six hundred feet.

"Also, Caleb doesn't keep any food in the cabin. That's to keep black bears and other animals from breaking in. What we bring in, we pack out!"

"Thank you Shana, great info!" Mandi said. "Now food. What do we take for two dinners, two breakfasts, and one lunch?"

Chris added, "There's a great REI store in Burlington, in the next town over. We can get anything we need for hiking and food. And if anyone needs camping gear, they'll have it."

The rest of the afternoon and evening was spent getting to know one another and making the run to Burlington for supplies.

**Scene Two: Sunday — The Voyage to Sequim**

They all had breakfast at the house at five sharp and then adjourned to the Nordic Tug garage mooring.

Chris was very familiar with the thirty-seven-foot tug; he had cruised the Sound regularly in a Nordic. He briefed everyone on the operation and safety features, then reviewed the morning forecast: cloudy, Sea State 3, with two- to four-foot chop.

"Well, gang," Chris said in his best naval voice, "our cruise will be on a typical Puget Sound fall day. Misty, sometimes foggy. We'll need sharp eyes—cargo ships, oilers, ferries. All ships follow the rules of the road for inland waters except private boats piloted by people who think they're admirals on a carrier."

He assigned lookout duties, then smiled. "Let's avoid getting into extremis. Cast off!"

The tug eased out into Padilla Bay and threaded through Guemes Channel.

The run toward Sequim wasn't bad. Some chop, but manageable. As they neared Sequim Bay, the sky began to clear.

"This is Sequim's gift to the Peninsula," Shana said, gesturing toward the horizon. "The Blue Hole."

"What's the Blue Hole?" Mandi asked.

Chris eased back on the throttle as the tug slipped into Sequim Bay, the water flattening into a peculiar, luminous calm.

"That darker patch out there," he said, nodding toward an oval of deep blue just offshore, "that's the Blue Hole. A glacial cut drops off fast. Cold water wells up from below, and the currents behave differently there. They pull instead of drift. Locals don't swim it, and boats don't linger."

He glanced up at the sky, now improbably bright. "Same geology gives Sequim its weather. The Olympic Mountains split storms coming in off the Pacific. Most of the rain dumps on the west side, and what's left dries out by the time it reaches us. That's the rain shadow."

He smiled slightly. "A lot of commercial airline pilots keep homes here. After flying through gray skies all week, they come to Sequim to remember what the sun looks like."

They docked just after noon.

As Chris secured the last line, Shana glanced toward the wooden sign at the head of the dock, **JOHN WAYNE MARINA.** The letters weathered but proud.

"Wayne kept a place up here," she said. "A house outside town. A boat in the harbor. He loved Sequim because it stayed out of the spotlight—sunny, quiet, practical. When the marina was built, the locals named it after him not because he was famous, but because he understood the place."

She smiled. "You come here to work, to heal, or to disappear for a while. He did all three."

Shana looked up from the road and smiled. "Uncle Caleb."

They greeted one another warmly, and Caleb suggested lunch first. Over cod and chips at the snack shack, he laid out the plan for the hike and the overnight stay at the cabin where they'd stop, what they'd carry, and what the forest would tolerate.

When the plates were cleared, Caleb reached into his jacket and unfolded a sheet of paper worn soft at the creases. He smoothed it flat on the table, anchoring one corner with his thumb.

"Before we walk into it," he said, "you should understand what you're about to see."

He glanced at each of them once, then back to the drawing.

"This is the Pacific Yew. Once we get into the forest I will give you a more comprehensive briefing.

## Scene Three: Sunday Afternoon — Into the Forest

After lunch they drove to the upper Dungeness trailhead, pavement giving way to gravel, gravel to forest. At the trailhead, they unloaded and walked single file beneath towering cedars.

"This is Pacific Yew country," Caleb said, slowing as they entered the darker tree covered trail.

He pointed out the Pacific Yew tree. Smaller than the firs around it, the yew seemed almost withdrawn—needles darker, posture patient.

He brought out the diagram again and gave a more in-depth briefing using the drawing and actual tree to illustrate his words.

"People think it's rare because it hides." He said. "Truth is, it survives by not drawing attention."

He brushed a branch where a few red arils hung, barely visible in the shade.

"The red skin isn't poison," he said. "It's a carrier. The seed inside is toxic."

## VARIANT A

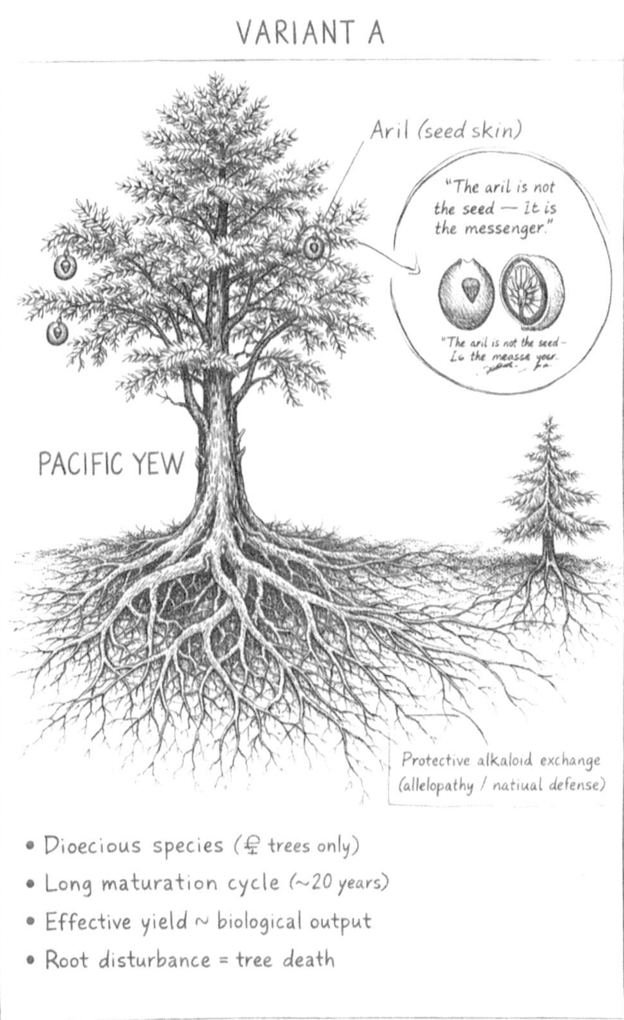

"What limits the yew isn't its ability to fruit," he continued. "It's what survives long enough to become the next tree. Birds take most. Rot takes some. Shade claims others. Successful regeneration takes time."

"How long?" Mandi asked.

"Twenty years to maturity," Caleb said. "That's the rhythm."

He started walking again.

"When the cancer pharmaceutical paclitaxel hit the market, the bark was the raw material. That usually killed the tree. And no one wanted to wait twenty years to replace it."

Chris nodded. "I remember. The media called them the bark years."

"Permits. Quotas. Corporate contracts," Caleb said. "James Pharmaceuticals was one of the manufacturers. Not the worst, but they were in it."

He rested his hand briefly on the trunk of a yew.

"The tree paid for our impatience," he said. "That's the part people forget."

He straightened. "The rest of the story needs a fireplace."

## Scene Four: Sunday Night — Caleb's Cabin

The cabin was simple. Cedar walls darkened by decades of smoke, a stone fireplace radiating slow, even heat. Outside, the forest had gone still.

They ate dehydrated stew and cornbread from mismatched enamel bowls. Hunger made everything taste better.

"The bark stripping years were driven by urgency," Caleb said. "The medication worked. Cancer didn't wait. Neither did the industry. They adjusted."

He poked the fire once, sending sparks up the chimney. "Semi-synthetic methods eased the bark pressure later. Helped save what was left. But they didn't erase the damage."

"People remember the miracle," Mandi said softly. "They forget the cost."

Across the room, Shana shifted closer to the hearth. Chris noticed without thinking, resting his hand lightly at the small of her back. She leaned into it.

"The yew survives," Caleb said, "because it never puts everything in one place. It spreads risk. Time. Energy. It assumes loss."

"Tomorrow," Mandi said, "we learn the science."

Caleb nodded. "Tomorrow you learn what can be measured. Tonight is for remembering why restraint matters."

**Scene Five: Monday — The Grove Lessons**

Morning light filtered through the grove in long, angled shafts. Caleb led them slowly.

"The yew isn't rare," he said. "It's particular. It lives under protection— older trees, deeper shade. Too much sun and it weakens. Too much attention and it disappears."

"The yew trees produce arils across their lifetimes," he continued. "Some years none. Some years a handful. What survives does so by chance as much as design."

They spoke of toxicity, of chain of custody, of the difference between science and greed.

By afternoon, Mandi's notebook was full.

That night, back at the cabin, no one felt the need to add more words. The grove had given them more than data, it had given them responsibility.

**Scene Six: Tuesday — The Return**

At dawn they packed. Before leaving, Shana asked to take a small sample for Danny.

Caleb selected a young yew, cutting a narrow strip of bark and a small bundle of needles. "That's enough," he said. "Honor the tree."

They hiked out, returned to Sequim, and cast off by noon. By late afternoon, Anacortes came into view and the Nordic Tug slid home into its berth.

Three days had changed them.

As they secured the tug, Mandi noticed the Cessna in the hangar. She found Skip on the deck.

"JP asked me to bring the plane back," Skip said. "He's flying into SeaTac tonight."

Later that evening, when JP arrived from his meeting at the Pentagon, Mandi and JP retreated upstairs.

"I missed you," he whispered.

"Being married really is better," she murmured.

Outside, the Sound settled into night. In the morning, they would all meet again at NinthWave HQ. One step closer to the Pentagon, and one step deeper into the long shadow cast by the forest.

# CHAPTER 8

# Visit to The Pentagon
# Washington, DC

**Scene One: Korean War Veterans Memorial, Early Monday Morning**

I woke before dawn, still on Pacific time. I had arrived the night before from San Francisco, eaten a light dinner, and gone to bed at the Marriott by the Mall. I knew I had to be sharp for my 1000 hours meeting at the Pentagon. I wasn't sure what my role would be, so with Skip's help, I had prepared a PowerPoint presentation; The commercial overview of the current burn market. Admiral Albert hadn't been very specific, only that the meeting involved burns and troop rotation. I was as prepared as I could be without knowing the exact subject.

I dressed in my best military–civilian business suit, had breakfast at the hotel, bought a *Washington Post*, and stepped into the warm, gray fall morning. I walked toward the Washington Monument and then on to the Korean War Veterans Memorial. A light fog drifted off the Potomac and curled along the Mall, wrapping the monuments in a kind of waking silence.

By the time I reached the Korean Memorial, the air was thick. Nineteen soldier statues stood in formation, ponchos caught in a phantom wind, faces drawn and alert. Mist clung to their helmets and pooled at their boots. They looked as if they had been moving all night and had just turned to watch me.

I circled slowly among them, the gravel damp underfoot, their reflections faint on the slick granite wall. The etched faces there seemed to breathe with the fog. like ghosts meeting their steel counterparts in the mist.

Down by the Pool of Remembrance, I stopped. The water was still, dark as oil, the flag above it hanging limp. A low granite wall rimmed the pool, beaded with moisture. That was where the *Post* came in handy. It wasn't for the headlines. I folded it twice, laid it across the stone, and sat down, my suit remaining dry.

The granite was cold even through the paper, but it anchored me. Across the pool the soldiers stood half-lost in fog, their reflections wavering. I sat quietly, breathing with the mist, thinking about war and the men I had served with on the Destroyers years after the Korean War—the ones who came home and the ones who didn't.

Duty changes shape, but it never really ends.

Somewhere behind me a flag halyard clicked in a slow rhythm. The city was waking, traffic beginning on the bridge. But here, time was still. A pause between memory and whatever waited ahead.

I thought about the human and financial cost of war. No matter the scope, it seemed to me, a retired naval officer, a mystery of reasoning. Wars were once fought for territory and resources needed for survival. Japan was the perfect example; they had no domestic oil and fought for access to it. Now wars were too often driven by politics, greed and power. But what about the men and women who did the fighting? What was their gain?

I was not anti-war. I believed that the strongest offense possible is the best defense. I had dedicated my life to helping people, and today I had an opportunity to help both warriors and civilians increasingly caught in conflicts driven by ambition and fear.

I closed my eyes, bowed my head, and thought about the fighters, no matter what side they were on. I said a silent prayer that NinthWave would find answers. Not answers to war itself that the burden belonged to the Pentagon, but answers to the pain and disfigurement war leaves behind.

When the first light caught the far wall of the Pentagon, I folded the damp paper, slipped it under my arm, and stood. The seat of my trousers was dry enough for a briefing. I buttoned my suit coat and took one last look at the soldiers in the mist.

"At ease, boys," I murmured. "I'll take the watch for a while."

Then I turned toward the river and started walking.

## Scene Two - Pentagon — Monday Morning, 0945 hours

The Pentagon

I left the memorial at 0900 hours, just as the sun broke through the fog over the Potomac. The walk across the Arlington Bridge felt longer than it was. Halfway over, I flagged a cab heading toward the Pentagon. The driver didn't talk, and I didn't need him to. The city was waking behind me; ahead, the morning briefings were already underway.

The cab dropped me at the main entrance off Route 27, the riverside. The Pentagon rose out of the morning haze like a fortress from another time: five sides of pale limestone, precise and imposing, the flag at half-staff from last week's memorial. The driver pulled to the curb, and I stepped out, briefcase in hand.

I still remembered the smell of waxed floors, old paper, and the faint ozone of too many fluorescent lights. I'd worked here years ago when I was in the active Naval Reserve. For two weeks of every year, I was attached to the Assistant Secretary of Health for the DoD.

"E-Ring," it was called. It had been a while, and I'd almost forgotten how you actually got there. I never used the elevators. The Pentagon was a labyrinth of ramps, not stairs. The building's strange grace, sloping inward and outward like a great concrete ship.

At the security desk, I presented my retired officer's ID and the special clearance letter Admiral Brewer had sent me. The guard checked the list, compared the barcode, and gave a short nod.

"Welcome back, Captain," he said, sliding the visitor badge across the counter. "Escort's waiting past the turnstile."

I clipped the badge to my lapel, passed through the scanner, and entered the long corridor. The hum of the building was immediate — shoes on tile, murmured voices, the low percussion of a place that never slept.

The escort, a young Lieutenant in a crisp Navy uniform, fell in beside me. "Good morning, sir. Secretary's suite is down this way. We'll take the inner ramp to the E-Ring."

The ramps came back to me as soon as we started — polished concrete, gentle grade, the smell of coffee drifting from an open office door. I could almost hear my younger self walking these halls — the rhythm of service, the shorthand of acronyms, the weight of responsibility that hung heavier here more than anywhere else in Washington, D.C.

We reached a broad corridor lined with framed photos of past battle groups. The corridor opened into the E-Ring, the Navy's side, where light from small high windows spilled across the tile in geometric patches.

We reached the door marked **#500 — Office of the Assistant Secretary of Defense for Health Affairs**.

I thanked the Lieutenant and straightened my tie. The old instincts kicked in, shoulders back, face composed. I'd been here before, but this time the stakes were different. NinthWave wasn't the Navy, but today our work would carry the same weight.

**Scene Three: Pentagon — Admiral Brewer's Office, Monday 0955 hours**

I arrived at Vice Admiral Brewer's office precisely at 0955. His aide checked my badge and waved me through.

Brewer stood behind his desk, jacket off, coffee untouched beside a folder stamped **BURN PROGRAM — TOP SECRET**.

"Right on time, JP," he said, glancing at his watch. "Good to have you back in the building."

He gestured me to a chair. "We brief the team at 1015 hours, but I wanted to align expectations first."

He studied me for a moment, not as an administrator, but as someone weighing risk.

"You and Mandi have built something unusual at NinthWave. Ethnopharmacology, thermal-stable compounds, unconventional sourcing. That's why you're here."

He didn't soften the words. "Burn injuries are costing us readiness. Not just soldiers, civilians. Entire populations, now. We need solutions that don't exist yet."

He slid a thin dossier across the desk.

"You'll be working with General Hank McKenna, logistics and troop-rotation modeling, and Dr. Emily Vargas, one of the country's top burn and reconstructive specialists. They know your background. Today is about deciding whether this becomes a contract."

Brewer stood. "Let's meet the team."

**Scene Four: Pentagon — Secure Conference Room, 1018 hours**

General Hank McKenna didn't waste time.

He stood at the lectern like a field commander briefing a map — calm, precise, economical.

"Burns remove personnel longer than any other survivable wound," he said. "That's the problem."

The slide behind him showed a single chart.

"In the last decade, burns accounted for roughly three percent of battlefield injuries. Missile-era warfare doubles that, sometimes triples it. Recovery times stretch from weeks to months. Some never return."

He clicked again. "Every thousand burn casualties costs roughly ninety thousand troop-days. Rotation delays average three and a half weeks. Re-enlistment drops by more than sixty percent after severe burns."

He paused, letting the numbers sit.

"We've improved surface care. We haven't solved penetration. No field-ready agent reaches damaged sub-dermal tissue. Every hour before evacuation compounds the injury."

I leaned forward. "General, does that data reflect today's conflicts? Drone and missile warfare?"

McKenna nodded. "Ukraine changed the math. Burns now represent up to nine percent of injuries. Deeper, chemically contaminated, often sealed by residue. Worse, civilians are now the majority."

He brought up a final image of urban casualty overlays. "In hybrid warfare, burns stop being a military injury. They become a civilian catastrophe. Three civilians for every soldier. Mortality rates triple without advanced care."

Admiral Brewer folded his hands. "That's why NinthWave matters," he said quietly. "This isn't just readiness anymore."

Dr. Vargas reached for the remote.

**Scene Five: Pentagon — Secure Conference Room, 1040 hours**

Dr. Emily Vargas — Deep Burn Pathophysiology

"We can manage burns," Vargas said. "We can't regenerate them."

She displayed a simple cross-section of skin. "Once a burn crosses roughly four millimeters, the microvascular network collapses. Oxygen stops. Fibroblasts die. Below that depth, the tissue becomes biologically inert."

She tapped the gray layer. "No compound, pharmaceutical, biologic, or cellular reliably reaches that zone intact."

Another slide appeared, missile-burn pathology. "Missile and drone burns add a chemical seal. Metal oxides and residues cap the wound, blocking oxygen and drug penetration. The tissue often dies inward for days, even after debridement."

Her voice remained clinical, but the implication was stark. "We've tried stem cells. Growth factors. Nanocarriers. Hyperbarics. Everything that stimulates regeneration self-destructs before it reaches the target layer."

She shut off the projector. "The science has plateaued. What we lack is a compound that survives heat, penetrates depth, and remains biologically active."

Brewer turned toward me. "JP. That's why you're here."

## Scene Six: Pentagon — Secure Conference Room, 1055 hours

Dr. Jean Paul Kornig — NinthWave Briefing

I stood and brought up the NinthWave crest. "The global burn-care market spends billions," I said. "Less than ten percent goes toward deep-tissue solutions. Most products still target surface wounds technologies developed decades ago."

Logos appeared briefly, then disappeared.

"They work in hospitals. They fail in heat, dust, and kinetic trauma. None are field-grade."

I advanced the slide. "The gap is consistent across industry: No penetration beyond two millimeters. Thermal instability above forty-two degrees Celsius. Short shelf life. Poor adaptability across military and civilian use."

I paused. "In humanitarian zones, one compound must treat soldiers, civilians, and animals alike. The market doesn't design for that reality."

The final slide showed a simple diagram, DoD, academia, industry. "Our proposal is straight forward. Defense defines the requirement. Science develops heat-stable carriers. Industry scales under controlled IP."

I closed the laptop. "The data shows urgency. NinthWave exists to close that gap."

Brewer nodded once. "This gives us the framework we need."

**Scene Seven: Pentagon — Secure Conference Room, 1200 hours**

Brewer folded his hands. "We'll proceed toward a one-year discovery contract. Scope of Work finalized within a week. Funding is available."

Emily outlined clinical benchmarks.

Hank specified rotation metrics.

When it was my turn, I said, "Freedom to operate under a defined protocol. Monthly transparency. Early termination if objectives prove unattainable with proportional compensation."

Brewer smiled faintly. "That's how discovery contracts should be written."

They agreed.

As the others departed for lunch, Brewer held me back.

"This will be Top Secret. No leaks. No speculation. I trust your security team."

"You know Peter Peterson," I said.

Brewer nodded. "Enough said."

He slipped the classified folder under his arm. "Let's eat before the Navy beans disappear."

That night, I attended the Washington Symphony, Holst's *The Planets*. Mars sounded different after a day spent discussing fire.

The next afternoon, I flew back to Seattle.

The work had begun.

# CHAPTER 9

# Meeting of the Ninthwave Team

**Anacortes, WA — Wednesday, 9:00 AM**

The team gathered on the deck of NinthWave HQ at 9:00 AM. A light breakfast, hot coffee, and a few minutes to settle in helped everyone get reacquainted. Around the table were Mandi and I, Skip, Danny, Shana, and Chris.

"Shana," I said, "I see your dad came in over the weekend and divided the Great Room into two spaces; one for NinthWave HQ and one for relaxation. As we used to say in the Navy Bravo Zulu. Well done! "

Shana smiled. "Thank you, JP. He's proud you've included Danny and me."

"Good," I said. "Let's move inside."

As we climbed the short stairs from the deck to the HQ entrance, Mandi leaned in and whispered, "JP, you're not at the Pentagon today. You can ease off the command posture."

I felt my face warm. "Of course, Mandi."

**Scene One — NinthWave HQ Suite**

We gathered around a boardroom-style table facing a wall-length video screen. Skip had wired the room so completely that any device could project with a single tap.

I slid a fob into my laptop. The title slide appeared immediately in stark, uncompromising black:

**TOP SECRET — FOR YOUR EYES ONLY — NOFORN**

"I realize Skip and I are the only ones here who personally hold this clearance," I began. "However, all of you are operating under an umbrella access structure, with Skip and me as the accountable officers. That allows us to brief, plan, and work together on this venture while responsibility for security remains with us."

Chris spoke first. "So that means this venture; what it is, who it involves, and anything derived from it stays inside this circle? No written, spoken, electronic, or visual communication beyond the team. Correct?"

"Exactly," I said. "Everyone tracking so far?"

Shana raised a hand. "How do we talk to each other, and how do we get information from people not on the team?"

"Good question," I replied. "Inside this group, communication is unrestricted. Outside this group, the rule on the screen applies—absolute containment. We may collect information externally, but nothing about why or how we're doing this leaves the room."

I looked around the table. "Do you all understand and agree?"

Each person nodded.

Danny asked quietly, "And if someone violates the rule?"

I answered without humor. "Then the contract collapses. Funding disappears. Careers can be damaged. More importantly, science intended to heal could be repurposed to harm."

Skip leaned forward. "In the 1990s, satellite engineers shared post-launch data with China—just a few equations. It improved missile guidance accuracy and triggered international hearings. Small leaks can shift global balances."

I nodded. "Classification isn't about secrecy for its own sake. It's about preventing good science from becoming a weapon in the wrong hands."

No one moved. No one opted out.

"Good," I said. "Let's begin!"

**Internal Briefing — NINTHWAVE PENTAGON VENTURE
Prepared by Dr. Jean Paul Kornig, PharmD, FASCP, FHIMSS**

Slide 1 — Security Covenant
TOP SECRET — FOR YOUR EYES ONLY — NOFORN
- Absolute prohibition on external communication
- Historical precedent: Long March technology transfer (1998)
- Purpose: protect discovery, prevent adversarial exploitation
- Team security covenant affirmed

Slide 2 — Pentagon Counterpart Team
- Vice Admiral Brewer — Assistant Secretary of Defense, Health Affairs
- Brigadier General Hank McKenna — Combat Health Logistics
- Dr. Emily Vargas — Burn & Reconstructive Medicine
  - University of Texas Houston Burn and Reconstruction Center
  - Memorial Hermann John S. Dunn Burn Center
- Dr. Jean Paul Kornig — NinthWave Lead

**Operational Axes:** policy • logistics • science • application

Slide 3 — Scientific Reality (Vargas)
- No validated regenerative therapy beyond ~4 mm depth
- Missile/drone burns form a chemical "cap" blocking oxygen and absorption
- Existing agents fail due to heat degradation or delayed healing

**Requirement:** heat-stable, deep-penetrating regenerative compound

Slide 4 — Readiness Impact (McKenna)
- Burns ≈ 2.6% of battlefield casualties; ~50% severe
- Recovery timelines: 18–240 days
- Drone-era warfare doubles burn incidence
- Civilian casualties now exceed military by 3:1

**Core Thesis:** Readiness begins with recovery.

Slide 5 — Brewer's Mandate
- Field-stable therapeutic agent
- ≥50% reduction in recovery time
- Dual-use: military and civilian
- Absolute operational security

**Directive:** Make regeneration operational.

Slide 6 — Target Outcomes
- Tissue penetration ≥4 mm
- Regeneration, not stabilization
- Prototype within 12 months
- Protected intellectual property
- Day-90 compound screening data

Slide 7 — Operating Principles (Kornig)
- Freedom of discovery; no micromanagement
- Transparent oversight and reporting
- Ethical integrity; voluntary exit permitted
- Early termination if objectives prove unattainable

**Unified Mission:** End burn suffering.

Final Slide
*Ninth Wave Crest — the breaking wave on white*
*From Battlefield to Healing Field*
*— The Ninth Wave Response*

### *Discussion Break*

"After lunch," I said, "we'll hear the Pacific Yew team's report and see whether what they observed in the field may suggest a direction aligned with the regeneration problem we're facing."

"Lunch will be catered from Gere-a-Deli. Use this room. Skip and I will be on the deck. Mandi, join us once the teams are settled."

**Scene Two — Pre-Lunch Security Conversation (Deck)**
Skip, Mandi, and I stepped onto the deck overlooking Padilla Bay. A faint breeze carried salt and cedar.

"Here's the situation," I said. "We've got the bull by the horns, and he's charging the wall! We need to wrestle him down before we get there."

"Well said," Skip and Mandi replied together.

"First'security," I continued. "P² at TNIC is building the new communications stack, the Quantum Whisper Bridge."

Skip nodded. "He's been waiting years for a real use case. Now he has one. When I get back to Mammoth, we'll have a working version. Secure lines, rotating quantum keys, undetectable traffic patterns."

"Good," I said. "Now Mandi, how did Sequim go?"

She smiled. "Very smooth. The Nordic ran perfectly, and Caleb was more helpful than I expected. Nothing definitive, but after hearing your Pentagon brief, I'm starting to have a glimmer."

"Let it play out," Skip said. "Right now the page is blank."

"It may not be the answer," Mandi said. "But it's a direction."

As Mandi went inside, Skip nudged me. "You've got a winner there, old buddy."

"You're right!" "I say that every day."

# CHAPTER 10

## Pacific Yew Trip Brief

**Anacortes, WA — Wednesday, 1:00 PM**

**Scene One — Lunch / Pacific Yew Debrief**

The team drifted back into the NinthWave HQ suite with paper plates and steaming cups of soup. Dill from the Gere-a-Deli sandwiches floated through the room. Sprawled across the table were maps of the Pacific Yew Grove, green corridors laid out like a secret topography. Chris set his field notebook beside the projector.

Mandi tapped the opening slide.

**Yew Grove Recon: Findings & Next Steps**

"Shana," she said. "Take us through it."

Shana raised the clicker and began.

**Slide 1 — Agenda**

Sunday
- Nordic Tug to Sequim ~6–7 hrs, weather dependent
- Moored at John Wayne Marina
- Picked up by Caleb — drive to trailhead
- Hike to cabin
- Overnight in cabin

Monday
- Full day in the Pacific Yew Grove
- Yew ecology, growth cycles, historical context

Tuesday
- Return to Anacortes

She answered questions as they came, then clicked ahead.

**Slide 2 — Pacific Yew History**
- Ancient understory forest ecology
- Bark-stripping era and black-market impact
- Discovery of cancer compounds
- Parallel pharmaceutical development in the U.S. and Russia
- Shift to semi-synthetic Taxol
- Toxicity of needles, bark, and roots
- Twenty-year growth cycle and supply constraints

She paused before the final slide.

**Slide 3 — Conclusions**
- Pacific Yew remains a powerful medicinal plant
- Bark-derived cancer medications were developed by James Pharmaceutical (U.S.) and Vostapex (Russia)
- Long maturation cycles — scarcity — illegal harvesting
- All parts except the aril are clinically toxic
- Drug selectively targets malignant cells

Shana lowered the clicker. Silence settled over the room.

### *Mandi's Reflection*

"Shana captured everything," Mandi said. "But after hearing Dr. Vargas's Pentagon report, I'm not convinced the yew is our production path. It's slow, poisonous, temperamentally fragile. This isn't a product-development project, this is a Discovery Venture.

"We need a plant that's safe, renewable, scalable. Something that grows in years, not decades."

She let the thought settle.

"So…is this where the yew leads us? Or is this where our search begins?"

The room remained still until Danny spoke.

### Danny's Tale

Danny cleared his throat quietly, but with intent.

"I'm the newbie here, the new thinker. I don't carry old assumptions. But I did create a burn salve from the Pacific Yew, and even if it isn't the Pentagon solution, it taught me something worth remembering."

He leaned forward, elbows on the table.

"Caleb and I used to guard the grove during bark-stripping season; long nights, shotguns across our laps, mugs of beer cooling on the porch rail. We didn't own those trees, James Pharmaceutical did. Yet, when a twenty-year yew died from over-stripping, we felt it in our guts. Watching a tree die that slowly…it's like watching a library burn!"

No one spoke.

"The yew already gave us one miracle…the cancer drug. So we started wondering: if its poisons protect the tree, could a controlled form protect flesh? Could the thing that defends the forest defend us too?"

He let the question breathe.

"We studied everything; needles, bark, cambium, seeds, but the real secret was in the root mat. A world beneath the soil where the tree communicates, defends, and survives. That's where the chemistry hides-subtle, complex, ancient. The fireworks salve came from that root-bed work."

### The Ancient Myth

"You know," Danny continued, "the Pacific Yew's story didn't start in Washington. It goes back at least thirteen thousand years. Before there were groves here, there were groves in what's now Siberia. Same genus. Same toxins. Same resilience.

"Oral histories speak of an extinct Siberian tribe who brewed a root tea used only during rites of passage. They called themselves something that roughly translates to 'the people who walk the world upside down.' Outsiders later twisted it into a nickname: the Hopped-Up Upside-Downs.

"Was the tea psychoactive? Probably. Was it medicinal? Almost certainly. The chemistry suggests root alkaloids capable of leaving long-lasting biochemical signatures."

Danny's voice stayed even.

"But the tribe harvested whole roots. They killed their groves. And when the yew vanished, so did they. One elder, (according to the story) crossed the land bridge into Alaska carrying dried bark and seeds. Whether those seeds survived is unknown, but the migration pattern of yew in North America doesn't fully match climate models alone. Something or someone, helped it along."

He sat back.

"The lesson the yew taught them is the same lesson it's teaching us: If you take without restraint, the forest disappears. If you listen, it offers wisdom."

### Skip's Analysis

Skip finally exhaled. "Danny…that's a hell of a story. The engineer in me wants to label half of it folklore. But the systems guy in me, knows stories aren't random. Stories are data encoded observations."

"Exactly," I said. "Which brings us to next steps."

### AI Pathway Investigation

"Skip," I said, "run a deep analysis. Feed everything"the myth, the Siberian lineage, environmental parallels into P²'s Scenario engine.

Cross-reference ethnobotanical archives, migration patterns, and root-usage records. Let Q'ARIUM tell us whether this is myth, or memory."

Mandi added, "And if something matches the chemistry?"

"Then," I said, "we'll know the Hopped-Up Upside-Downs weren't just a campfire story."

Skip nodded. "Understood."

### *Assignments & Sub-Groups*

I stood.

"We split into teams."

**Pacific Yew Group** (future involvement assumed)
- Danny — Lead chemist
- Shana — Field analysis
- Chris — Plant science
- Caleb — Culture, stewardship

Goal: Deconstruct the Fireworks Salve; identify root-system chemistry; evaluate real burn-healing potential

**Production Review (Cancer-Line Products)**
- Mandi — Lead
- Chris backup
- Audits at James Pharmaceutical & Danube
- Liaison with Georg Messinger, Danube CEO
Goal: Understand vulnerabilities, ethics, and legacy supply chains

**TNIC & Security**
- Skip — Lead
- Scenario analysis and the Quantum Whisper Bridge (QWB)
Goal: Secure data; map ethnochemical pathways

**Executive & Pentagon Interface**
- JP — Lead

Goal: Manage Pentagon discussions; apply findings clinically; guide venture trajectory

***The NinthWave Discovery Protocol Stages***
Identify Clinical Need
Map Market Horizon
Assess Existing Therapies
Measure NinthWave Capabilities
Research & Discovery
Feasibility Ranking
Go / No-Go Review
Development Plan
Implementation & Monitoring

"This isn't bureaucracy," Mandi said. "It's strategy."

Danny smiled. "And it keeps us from inventing a new religion!"

***Schedule***

"Thursday through Tuesday," I said, "we work our assignments. Wednesday is HQ review. If the Pentagon calls, I fly Monday and return Tuesday."

Skip nodded. "That works."

Mandi looked around the table. "Week One begins now."

The team gathered their notebooks as amber light spread across Padilla Bay. For the first time, NinthWave wasn't just studying the unknown, they were stepping into it deliberately.

# CHAPTER 11

# Implementation of the Discovery Protocol

**Anacortes — Thursday Morning**

**Scene One — Padilla Bay Morning**

Dawn rose pale and cold over Padilla Bay. The house was quiet except for the hum of the espresso machine and the soft rustle of briefing pages curling at their edges—remnants of yesterday's marathon session. By morning, the NinthWave team had already dispersed along four distinct paths.

Skip departed late Wednesday night, heading down the stairs to the hangar with a backpack slung over one shoulder.

"TNIC's Scenario engine and I have a date with history," he said, offering a half-salute.

By sunrise, he was already in Mammoth, deep inside the TNIC facility with Peter Peterson P², preparing the first tranche of scenario inputs: Pacific Yew lineage data, taxane chemistry, Siberian migration patterns, ethnobotanical burn lore, Indigenous root preparations, and anything that might illuminate a viable path forward.

As the Cessna lifted off last night, Mandi had called after him, "Try not to let the AI out think you!"

Skip had only grinned. "That ship sailed two versions ago."

Back out on the deck, Shana, Danny, and Chris loaded gear aboard the Nordic Tug. They were heading back to Sequim, where Caleb would guide them once again into the Pacific Yew Grove to deepen the investigation into the Fireworks burn salve.

"Weather's holding," Chris said, with his mug steaming in the cold air. "We'll be in the grove by noon."

Inside, Mandi prepared for a secure call with the Aretē Taxol division; first with Clay Brown at the James Seattle Taxol facility, then later with Georg Messinger in Vienna. She needed a full status review of the European Taxol pipeline, including legacy Russian sourcing, before the next Wednesday briefing.

The James/Aretē facility south of Seattle, a discreet building without signage, still housed legacy tooling for taxane derivatives.

Georg, with his precise German thoroughness, remained Aretē's principal liaison to TazNiva Biologics in the Ural Federal District. His annual audits were equal parts diplomacy, compliance, and quiet verification.

As for me, I would fly to Washington on Monday. Admiral Brewer and Dr. Vargas had requested a follow-up review of NinthWave's Discovery Protocol and any early leads. Brewer had also hinted that contractual discussions would deepen.

I took my coffee onto the deck and settled into the rocking chair.

Yesterday this venture was a slide deck, I thought. Today it's a mission. Be safe out there… every one of you.

## Scene Two — Skip / TNIC

Skip slept only a few hours, landing at Mammoth shortly after midnight. Driving from the airstrip to the TNIC compound, he placed a secure call to $P^2$.

"Early Friday," Skip said. "We start with everything; Pacific Yew, Taxol history, Russian supply chains, Siberian root brews, Indigenous burn remedies, ancient migration routes. Let the system hunt for patterns."

He paused, then added, "I don't know the right clues yet. But once we identify them, the Scenario engine will tell us which ones matter."

P² replied without hesitation. "Copy. Datasets will be preloaded."

## Scene Three — Mandi / Aretē Coordination

Mandi's morning began with a secure call to Philip Bradsmith, CEO of James Pharmaceuticals, now operating under the Aretē umbrella. She provided an update within classification constraints, then requested authorization to speak directly with Clay Brown, operations director at the Seattle plant.

Approval was granted.

Within minutes, a secure session was scheduled with Clay, followed by a second call with Georg Messinger in Vienna. The objective was clear: align European Taxol audits with NinthWave's evolving requirements and assess TazNiva's operational reliability amid growing geopolitical uncertainty.

All parties agreed to reconvene before the Wednesday review.

## Scene Four — Nordic Tug / Pacific Yew Grove

The Nordic Tug crossed the Sound at first light on Monday and docked.

Mandi, Shana, Danny, and Chris met Caleb at the dock, then drove inland before hiking back into the Pacific Yew Grove with daypacks and notebooks.

As they hiked, Shana and Chris pressed Danny and Caleb for specifics.

"What exactly did James Pharmaceutical harvest?" "How much bark? How many needles?" "What solvent systems were used in the early extracts?" "And the Fireworks salve; process steps, heat exposure, yields?"

Danny and Caleb answered as precisely as memory allowed. Some details were imperfect, half experimentation, half intuition, occasionally accidental, but every fragment mattered now.

Before the group set off deeper into the grove, Mandi pulled Chris aside.

"Find out everything about Fireworks," she said quietly. "Everything."

Later that afternoon, golden light filtered through the canopy as they crouched beside a living root mat. The soil seemed to breathe slow, and deliberate. It was the kind of place where chemistry waited, undisturbed, for someone willing to listen.

## Scene Five — JP / The Pentagon

I flew east Monday morning. By noon, I was walking the E-Ring toward Admiral Brewer's office.

Brewer greeted me with his usual calm authority. Dr. Vargas joined us moments later. Together, we reviewed the NinthWave Discovery Protocol, refining feasibility thresholds, early screening criteria, and the biochemical constraints imposed by deep missile burns.

I asked Vargas whether archived taxane research had ever hinted at dermal regeneration or thermal stability.

"I'll pull everything," she said. "There were obscure studies in the late nineties. Something may have been overlooked."

Brewer then invited me back into his office to address a different matter.

"JP," he said, "if this works, it will fundamentally alter military medicine. You'll comply with all security conditions, but I want clarity on commercialization."

He summoned a Pentagon attorney. One hour later, he placed a document in front of me.

**ADDENDUM A NinthWave–DoD Cooperative Research & Product Utilization Agreement (CRPUA)**
**Classification: TOP SECRET — NOFORN**

**Section 7.2 — Intellectual Property and Royalty Rights**

**Ownership and Disclosure** All inventions or biological formulations conceived or first reduced to practice under this Agreement remain the property of NinthWave Biobotanica™, Inc., are subject to immediate disclosure to the Department of Defense.

**Government License** The United States Government retains a non-exclusive, irrevocable, royalty-free license for defense and public-health use, including authorized third-party manufacture.

**Commercial Rights and Royalties** NinthWave retains full commercial rights to patent, license, and distribution for non-governmental applications. Royalties accrue to NinthWave and designated inventors pursuant to the Bayh–Dole Act (1980) and FAR 52.227-11

**Preferred Procurement and Access** NinthWave shall ensure product availability to the U.S. Government at preferred-cost levels and maintain readiness under established DoD requisition procedures.

**March-In Provision** The DoD may invoke, march-in rights in the event of national emergency or production failure.

**Statement of Understanding** This Agreement affirms a shared commitment between science and service, the partnership of innovation and duty. Discovery remains free; protection remains paramount.

— Dr. Jean Paul Kornig — VADM Albert Brewer, USN (Ret.)

Brewer looked up. "Is this acceptable?"

"It is, Admiral."

I then returned to Anacortes late Tuesday night, and slipped quietly into bed beside Mandi.

"Long trip?" she murmured.

"Too long."

I started to mention Wednesday's briefing, but she shifted closer, her hair brushing my shoulder.

"JP," she whispered, "are you really trying to talk business right now?"

I hesitated. "Maybe not."

She laughed softly when she felt bare skin beneath the covers.

"You're hopeless," she said. "Really JP, you're a devil."

"Guilty," I said, pulling her close.

For once, the day ended without strategy or science.
Just warmth.
And silence.
And enough.

# CHAPTER 12

## Discovery Protocol: Week One

### Anacortes — NinthWave HQ Conference Room

**Scene One — The Meeting**

One week into the NinthWave Discovery Protocol, we already felt late.

Not because deadlines were close, they weren't, but because urgency had arrived ahead of the calendar.

Morning returned us fully to the work we could no longer delay.

Mandi and I took our seats at the head of the table. The team looked as I felt: a mixture of fatigue, curiosity, and cautious excitement.

Time to begin.

"The Admiral and I have signed the NinthWave–Pentagon Discovery Agreement," I said. "We now have funding to carry out the research and to pay our team."

Relief moved through the room with smiles, quiet nods, a few soft claps.

"Mandi and I will meet with each of you individually tomorrow. I think you'll be pleased. But performance drives everything now. If we don't hit each Discovery Success Gate, none of this continues."

Hands lifted. I stopped them with a raised palm.

"Hold the questions. Let's get into the briefings. Danny, you're up first."

## Scene Two — Danny Whulshad's Report

Danny stood, rubbing the corner of a notepad with his thumb.

"I've shared all my notes from the two years I worked on the Fireworks burn salve," he began. "Full honesty—this wasn't formal lab science. It was bench-level work, driven by observation, experience, and more than a little trial and error."

A few chuckles eased the room.

He walked us through the yew methodically: bark chemistry, needle toxicity, the poisonous seed, and the single exception, the red aril that surrounds the seed and appears harmless to birds.

"For clarity," Danny said, glancing up, "there are no bulbs in the yew. What matters underground are root-crown nodal structures, the lignified junctions where fine roots converge and interface with fungal networks."

Chris nodded slightly.

Danny continued. "That's where things get interesting, not as a harvest target, but as a physiological signal."

He flipped to the first slide: a simplified root diagram.

"The Pacific Yew is an understory survivor. It doesn't compete by height or speed. It competes by chemistry and patience. Its roots integrate into the mycorrhizal network, exchanging stress signals, defensive compounds, and metabolic cues."

He paused, choosing his words carefully.

"Over decades, sometimes centuries, those roots don't accumulate chemistry so much as they stabilize it. Bark and needles respond fast. They spike. They crash. Roots change slowly. They smooth noise."

Mandi leaned forward. "So the roots matter, but not as a drug source."

"Exactly," Danny said. "They matter because they explain the tree's behavior."

Chris spoke up. "You're saying the yew protects other trees."

"Yes," Danny replied. "Indirectly. Chemically. Quietly. Its compounds discourage overreach from insects, fungi, even aggressive neighboring roots. It doesn't dominate the forest. It prevents collapse."

The room went still.

Danny added, "We need to be careful with language here. We call these compounds poisons, and they are. At the wrong dose, in the wrong context, they kill cells."

He looked around the table.

"But in the forest, they don't act like weapons. They act like boundaries. They don't wipe things out. They limit behavior. They protect space without conquest."

Mandi folded her arms. "So good and bad."

Danny nodded. "Exactly. Bad if you force them. Good if you respect them. That's the difference between poison and medicine-context, intent, and control."

He took a step back. "I'm not claiming the roots are our solution. I'm saying they explain why this tree survives and why rushing extraction destroys the very system that makes it work."

## Scene Three — Chris's Briefing

Chris stepped forward, precise and calm.

His sketches weren't art, they were anatomy: trunk layers, cambium rings, root–fungal interfaces. Living architecture.

He summarized without embellishment:
- Tremendous biochemical potential
- Nearly impossible to cultivate at scale
- Twenty-year growth cycle
- Harvesting disrupts the system that creates the chemistry
- Root networks are integral but non-extractive

"I'm not saying eliminate the yew," Chris said. "But if we commit to it, we accept its limits as part of the design."

A follow-on slide mapped the global production chain—James, Danube, TazNiva—highlighting geopolitical exposure, supply fragility, and concentration risk.

Skip's remote update followed: Q'ARIUM was nearly ready to initiate its first full Scenario App runs.

**Scene Four — Summary and Decision Tension**

I stood again.

"Here's Week One in a sentence: the Pacific Yew is promising, dangerous, and unproven."

No one disagreed.

"We'll continue for now," I said. "But we expand the candidate pool. We cannot rely on a single slow-growing, toxic species with no margin for error."

Mandi added, "The Pentagon has defined the clinical need. The market horizon is mapped. Next step: work with Dr. Vargas on the full clinical landscape, and have Q'ARIUM identify other botanical candidates that meet thermal stability and regenerative requirements."

Nods circled the table.

We outlined next tasks and support paths. Momentum was building, but so was the awareness that the yew might not be the destination, only the doorway.

Notebooks closed. Chairs slid back.

***Discovery Protocol — Updated Status***
Stage 1: Identify Clinical Need — Complete
Stage 2: Market Horizon — Complete
Stage 3: Assess Clinical Landscape — In Progress
Stage 4: NinthWave Capabilities — Under Review

Candidate Pool: One tree. No margin for error.

### *GO / NO-GO Marker*

"One last thing," I said. "Next Wednesday we vote on the Pacific Yew. GO or NO-GO."

Danny looked down. Chris folded his arms. Shana exhaled softly. Mandi watched me, unreadable.

"If this path is wrong, even if it's ancient, elegant, and compelling, we walk away. We owe that to the Pentagon, to burn victims, and to each other."

The room held still.

"Good work today," Mandi said quietly. "Rest if you can. Tomorrow begins Week Two."

We stepped outside into the cooling evening. Padilla Bay lay quiet beyond the deck, waiting.

And somewhere in that quiet, I knew: Next Wednesday wouldn't just decide the yew. It would decide how NinthWave moved forward.

# CHAPTER 13

## Alternative Candidates and Clinical Profiles

### Anacortes — Ninth Wave HQ

The next morning, Mandi and I sat on the deck in our rocking chairs, coffee cups warm in our hands, watching a pale ribbon of fog lift off Padilla Bay. The house felt unusually quiet as everyone scattered across their assignments. Each one carrying a piece of a puzzle none of us could yet see clearly.

"JP," Mandi said, "tell me the one thing that's bothering you. I'll tell you what is bothering me."

I nodded. "Fair. You first."

"My concern," she said, "is that we only have one candidate. No matter how promising the yew is, we can't stake a Pentagon contract, and the lives behind it on a single potential solution. We need a comparison table: multiple candidates, multiple paths."

"Agreed," I said. "My concern is different. I understand surface burn therapies, but missile burns are something else entirely. They go deep… and they don't stop. Before we layer chemistry onto chemistry, I need to understand the clinical battlefield."

Mandi's eyes sharpened. "Then we're looking at the same problem just from opposite ends."

## Scene One — Clinical Clarity

"Let's bring in Emily," I said. "We need her to walk us through the physiology of a missile burn: how it spreads, how it destroys tissue, how it differs from thermal and electrical trauma."

Mandi nodded. "Once we understand the injury, we can match candidates to reality. That's how we avoid chasing ghosts."

I keyed up the secure Quantum Whisper Bridge. A soft pulse of blue light rippled across the conference table. A moment later, Emily's image resolved to a crisp uniform, hair pinned back.

"JP, Mandi," she said. "Seven P.M. here in Texas. What can I do for you?"

"Education," I said. "The real physiology of a missile burn."

Emily leaned forward, the clinical seriousness settling into her eyes.

### *Emily's Explanation — The Anatomy of Destruction*

"Alright," she began. "A missile burn isn't heat. It's a compound weapon—thermal, chemical, pressure, and plasma ionization."

She held up a stylus and sketched quickly on her tablet.

"When the missile strikes, the plasma wave vaporizes the epidermis and drives energy deep in the dermis, subcutaneous tissue, sometimes into muscle and bone. What looks like a clean surface is misleading; underneath is a frontier of dying cells."

She paused.

"And the burn spreads. Not by blood flow, but by intracellular cascade. Every dying cell releases radicals, enzymes, acids. These attack their neighbors. The tissue keeps burning long after the flame is gone."

Mandi inhaled sharply. I understood her thought: a child hit by a drone, what chance would they have?

Emily continued.

"Compare that to:
- Firewood burns — surface, predictable.
- Electrical burns — deep but focal, with entry and exit wounds.
- Missile burns — systemic chaos.

"Missile burns overwhelm the body's ability to heal. The immune system goes into cytokine storm, vessels collapse, fibroblasts shut down. Regeneration simply… stops."

She looked directly at us.

"That's why soldiers don't die from the burn. They die from the biochemistry that follows."

Silence followed—heavy, necessary.

Mandi asked, "So current topical salves? What do they actually do?"

Emily sighed.

"They soothe. They protect. They stall bacteria. But they do not stop cell death. Silver sulfadiazine, hydrocortisone variants, even experimental hydrogels, they buy hours, not recovery."

She paused again.

"Oxygen therapy helps in some wounds, hyperbaric chambers in particular, but missile burns aren't oxygen-starved. They're drowning in radicals. Adding oxygen can accelerate chemical damage."

She leaned closer.

"We don't need more oxygen. We need containment. Something that tells the reaction to stop, cell by cell, layer by layer."

Behind her clinical precision, I saw the fatigue. The kind that comes only when science keeps losing.

"Emily," I said quietly, "Thank you for your help, you've shown us what medicine can't do. Now let's see what intelligence can."

I turned to Mandi. "Tomorrow, have Skip feed all this into TNIC's Q'ARIUM computer system. Cross-reactivity tables, oxidative cascade patterns, global patent filings, obscure botanical records—anything that might give us a foothold."

Mandi nodded. "I'll tell him to look for holes in the chemistry. That's where new compounds hide."

## Scene Two — The Deck, Later That Evening

After dinner, we returned to the deck. Mist drifted in from the bay, blurring the horizon.

"At first light," Mandi said, "we bring in Georg. Seven A.M. here, four P.M. in Vienna. Skip has him loaded on the Bridge."

I nodded. "Good. We'll brief Georg on everything—Discovery Protocol and early findings."

"We'll show the full team Wednesday," she said. "One room, multiple continents. The first real NinthWave Symposium."

She sipped her wine, thinking. "After the call, Chris and I will head down to the Seattle plant. I want to see what James Pharmaceutical kept alive… and what they quietly shut down."

"Perfect," I said. "Skip and TNIC will polish the historical scenario over the weekend. Reconstruction by Tuesday night, Symposium Wednesday."

Mandi looked out over the water, her voice soft but firm.

"And if the story raises more questions than answers?"

I smiled.

"Then we let the next wave carry us, and we keep searching."

# CHAPTER 14

# Russian Connection and the Taxol Supply Chain

**Scene One — Anacortes, NinthWave HQ, 7:00 AM PST**

JP and Mandi sat at the NinthWave conference table, steam rising from their coffee, eyes fixed on the Quantum Whisper Bridge (QWB) screen as Skip brought in the Vienna link.

Georg appeared; crisp suit, immaculate office behind him, and his smile came easily.

"It's been too long," he said. "How are things at Seneca Ranch?"

"Strong," JP replied. "Aretē and NinthWave just opened a new alkaloid laboratory. Pinella and Cam Williamson are running the facility."

Mandi added, "And we've secured a new Pentagon contract—TOP SECRET, NOFORN. That's why Skip installed the QWB for you. We needed a secure line to keep you looped in."

Georg nodded slowly. "Then I assume this briefing will be… different from the usual catch-up."

JP summarized the Pentagon venture; missile burns, regeneration goals, and why the Pacific Yew had become a candidate. Mandi followed with the global Taxol landscape and the critical role Danube played through their TazNiva Biologics Taxol supplier in the Urals.

"James in the U.S. and Danube in Europe developed their Taxol lines in parallel," she said, "Different regulatory paths, shared chemistry, separate supply chains. When we learned Danube was sourcing Russian

Yew-based material through TazNiva, we realized we needed your eyes on the ground."

Georg raised an eyebrow. "Are you collaborating with TazNiva on cancer formulations?"

"No," JP answered firmly. "We're exploring whether other parts of the yew—root, aril, or unknown alkaloids that could have relevance for missile burn treatment. TazNiva must not know this. Not even suspect."

He leaned in.

"We'd like you to make an inspection trip under the guise of routine quality review. Look, listen, observe. Do nothing that jeopardizes your relationship."

Mandi added, "Next Wednesday, 8:00 AM Pacific—5:00 PM Vienna— Skip will present a historical yew analysis to set context. Please be on that call. Afterward, we'll brief together."

Georg nodded. "Understood. Most communication with TazNiva has been through product managers, not the CEO. He's… old Soviet school. I'll proceed carefully."

"Good," JP said. "Flat sales hide deeper problems. Your visit could become pivotal."

"Then I'll prepare accordingly," Georg said. "Talk soon."

The screen faded, leaving the room unusually quiet.

### Scene Two — Danube Division, Vienna, 11:00 AM Local Time

Morning sun flashed across the Danube River, scattering light into Dr. Georg Messinger's office on the twenty-third floor of the Andromeda Tower.

The old and the new baroque Vienna to one side of the Danube, glass and steel Donau City on the other, reflected in his window. Between psyche and chemistry, he often thought, the distance was thin. Both could turn toxic when ignored.

A knock sounded. "Come in, Klara."

Klara Schreiber, RN, Product Manager for the European Taxol line branded, TOXYNE™, stepped inside.

"Guten Morgen, Dr. Messinger. Is there an issue with TOXYNE?"

"No," he said. "You're doing excellent work." Georg paused. "I realized I've never visited our partner plant in Yekaterinburg, Russia in the Ural mountains. I'm considering a trip, officially routine, unofficially overdue. Thoughts?"

Klara smiled. "You deserve a vacation. And… I think I can create a situation that needs your and their attention."

She placed several TazNiva charts reflecting their performance on the conference table:
- small variances in batch documentation
- gaps in shipment ID sequences
- irregular QC signature patterns

"Sloppy," Georg murmured. "Not dangerous, but unacceptable. Let's give them a nudge."

"You want them to think there's a defect?" Klara asked.

"No," he said. "I want them to think we are paying attention."

He hesitated, then added carefully, "We have a standing agreement with James. We share the global oncology market for this line. Sales are flat not because of demand, but because of raw material constraints. It may benefit Aretē if the James plant in Seattle produced for both divisions."

Klara's eyebrows rose. "That would make sense."

"And Klara…what we discussed is confidential."

"Natürlich," she said. "You can trust me."

"Draft the letter to the TazNiva CEO-courteous, technical, routine. Bring it to me before sending."

**Scene Three — Vienna, Evening**

An hour later, Klara returned with the draft letter to the CEO.

Georg read it, made one small edit removing a courtesy that suddenly felt unnecessary, and signed.

She transmitted it through standard channels, as instructed.

A few hours later—just after 7:00 PM—Georg's phone rang.

"Dr. Messinger," the building's security chief said, "a courier from the Russian Embassy is here with a sealed packet. Signature required."

"Scan it," Georg said. "If it's paper only, send him up."

The elevator chimed. The courier handed over a thick envelope embossed with TazNiva's seal.

Inside was a letter from Dr. Viktor Sergeyevich Baranov, CEO of TazNiva Biologics.

The letter was unsettlingly prompt.

Viktor's program for Georg's visit included:
- visa sponsorship through the Russian Embassy
- a structured two-day technical review
- a full-day plant tour and executive meeting
- optional rest accommodations outside the city
- assigned transportation and security liaison

Georg read it twice.

The speed was wrong.

The tone too smooth.

The hospitality… curated.

He scanned the document into the QWB archive and watched the green encryption light blink.

"Control," he murmured. "Always control."

Outside his window, the Danube shimmered, dividing the Vienna he trusted from a world that watched too closely.

**Scene Four — Seattle, James Taxol Plant, 10:00 AM PST**

Mandi and Chris drove south from Anacortes along I-5, traffic heavy but familiar.

"I've moved between forests and labs most of my life," Chris said. "This project feels larger than anything I've touched, but I don't yet understand why."

"You will," Mandi replied. "It felt the same for all of us."

They arrived at an anonymous steel-clad building located near SeaTac and marked simply JAMES.

Inside, Clay Brown—mid-fifties, rolled sleeves, tired eyes—greeted them.

"Welcome to the James–Aretē Taxol Facility," he said. "We don't get many visitors. Poison doesn't attract tourism."

Chris glanced around. "So what are you guarding?"

Clay grinned. "Poison and paperwork. Mishandled, either can kill you."

He led them through stainless-steel processing lines and sealed reactors.

Holding up a laminated chart, Clay said, "Early bark extraction required roughly three mature yew trees per patient. Twig-needle semi-synthetics improved yield, but required exponentially more biomass."

Chris frowned. "So scaling isn't a chemistry problem. It's a biology problem."

"Exactly," Clay said. "We've got idle fermenters and clean capacity. We could double output tomorrow, if the trees existed. But every kilogram must be verified. That's the choke point."

Mandi nodded. "So if corporate secured an additional documented supply…"

"We could run it," Clay finished. "No shortcuts. That's how this plant survived twenty years of scrutiny."

As they exited, Clay gestured at the unadorned exterior.

"Looks plain," he said. "But it runs clean. Like the yew—silent, slow, dangerous if you don't respect it."

They returned to the car and drove back to Interstate 5 as the gates slid shut behind them.

"The deeper we go," Mandi said quietly, "the more the yew resists being owned."

# CHAPTER 15

# The Whulshad Scenario App Summit

## TOP SECRET — NOFORN — FOR YOUR EYES ONLY

**Scene One: NinthWave HQ — Monday Morning, Two Days Before the Summit**

Mandi and I met early to make sure the plan for Wednesday's Summit was on schedule. A great deal had happened over the weekend, and we wanted to be certain nothing was overlooked. A checklist lay spread across the table.

"Mandi," I said, "let's make sure we're in accord with the objectives. With everything shifting these last few days, I am sure we don't want any surprises."

She looked thoughtful. "JP, the big question now is whether we continue pursuing the Pacific Yew as our solution or look for an alternative. With all the work this team has done, we're drifting toward an all-eggs-in-one-basket posture. You know better than anyone that's not a safe place to be with the Pentagon. If we fail, the project dies. But if the yew is the answer, we're far ahead of anyone else."

"I agree," I said. "That's the primary objective of the Summit is, Go or No-Go on the yew. We have today and tomorrow to prepare Skip and the TNIC Q'ARIUM Computer System for the Scenario App run. Let's make sure the team has uploaded everything into Q'ARIUM that QWB has already captured the info."

She scrolled through her tablet. "Alright. Here's our confirmed list for the 8:00 AM TNIC Q'ARIUM Scenario App Summit on Wednesday:"

- Dr. JP Kornig — NinthWave
- Amanda Kornig — NinthWave
- Skip Howard — The NinthWave Investigative Center (TNIC) / QWB Coordinator
- Dr. Georg Messinger — CEO, Danube Division (Aretē)
- Danny Whulshad — NinthWave Research
- Caleb Whulshad — NinthWave Research
- Chris Williamson — NinthWave Field Operations
- Cam Williamson — Seneca Ranch Alkaloid Lab
- Kenji Nacheda — CEO, Bandai Pharmaceuticals
- Shana Lawrence — NinthWave
- Karen Mitchell — TNIC / Burn-Market Consultant
- Dr. Emily Vargas — Pentagon Medical Research Group

"We should call Emily, Cam, and Nacheda now," Mandi said. "They'll need context, especially Nacheda, since it's midnight in Tokyo."

The call to Emily was brief; she was already enthusiastic and fully aligned.

We reached Cam next.

"Cam, it's Mandi and JP. We wanted to follow up on the Summit invite. You'll be on with us Wednesday?"

"Of course," he said. "Chris and I have been talking about the yew. He thinks we've underestimated the root mat—and maybe dismissed the aril skin too soon. He sent me about five pounds of root mat and arils that he got from Caleb. I wasn't trying to go rogue; we just thought it was worth exploring alkaloid extraction from the full seed and aril."

"You're never out of line when it's discovery," I said.

"Anything interesting so far?" Mandi asked.

"It's early," Cam replied, "but something's going on in that root bed. It's like the yew and the neighboring trees are in a chemical alliance. I'll have preliminary data for Q'ARIUM tomorrow."

"Perfect," I said. "See you on QWB, Cam."

After the call, I leaned back. "Skip, P², and Q'ARIUM have a lot to process before Wednesday. Let's bring Bandai in now."

The QWB link shimmered to life.

"Good morning, JP, Mandi," Kenji Nacheda said from Bandai, Japan. "Or perhaps good evening from my side."

"Nacheda-san," I said, smiling, "thank you for staying up so late."

"When Bandai can work with NinthWave," he replied, "time zones do not exist."

Mandi briefed him on the Discovery Protocol and the Pacific Yew hypothesis.

"Ah, the yew," he said softly. "Ichii, we call it here. Our founder, Dr. Nakasone-sensei, believed its toxins teach the body how to defend itself at the cellular level. It seems you are walking the same path."

"We'd like Bandai to join us," I said. "Your experience with alkaloid stabilization and delivery could matter greatly."

"This is appropriate," Nacheda said. "I will review the yew literature before the Summit. I look forward to Wednesday."

The call ended cleanly.

"He's still the same," I said. "Humble, brilliant, and already thinking ahead."

Mandi smiled. "Then we're ready."

**Scene Two: NinthWave Headquarters — The Summit Presentation**

The lights dimmed until the room became a soft blue chamber.

Q'ARIUM stirred with lights in its core shifting, like aurora trapped beneath glass. A low harmonic thrum vibrated through the table as the Quantum Whisper Bridge linked every remote participant: Georg in Vienna, Emily in Texas, Skip in Mammoth, Nacheda in Japan, and the local team gathered in Anacortes.

Skip's voice cut through the quiet.

"This is Q'ARIUM Scenario App Run 1.7—ethnopharmacologic reconstruction. Confidence index: sixty-eight percent. Interpretive. Not literal history, but pattern history derived from oral fragments, migration models, ancient flashback history, and botanical data."

Static drifted across the wall screen.

**Q'ARIUM RECONSTRUCTION**
**The Whulshad Lineage — Origin Hypothesis**
**Epoch: ~12,900 BP**
**Objective: Trace ancestral origins of the Fire Root tradition and yew lineage translocation.**

The QWB screen static resolved into a view of a frozen Siberian world.

**Scene Three: Q'ARIUM Reconstruction — The Whulshad Lineage**

*A HUT OF SNOW AND SMOKE. THE YEAR, ESTIMATED AT 12,000 YEARS AGO.*

The Siberian hut crouched low against the tundra, half-swallowed by snow. Reindeer hides stretched over a frame of bent saplings sagged under the weight of winter. Smoke leaked through a hole in the roof, carried sideways by the wind.

Inside, two brothers Arven and Viktor sat close to the dying fire embers.

They wore layered skins—reindeer and fox—stitched with bone needles, seams sealed with fat. Their boots were stiff with ice. Their breath rose in pale clouds, even indoors.

Their mother lay behind them, wrapped in her sleeping furs. She had been frozen dead since dawn.

Between her folded hands rested a small clay bowl. Inside were scarlet skins, thin and translucent.

Russian Yew Aril skins. Fire Root.

Arven, the elder, crushed the skins gently between his fingers. His hands were steady, but his jaw trembled. He poured hot water from a stone kettle into a horn cup. The liquid bloomed red, then darkened.

The brothers drank in silence.

The tea burned warmth into their chests, pushed back fear, sharpened thought. It did not numb grief, but it allowed them to stand inside without breaking.

Outside, the wind screamed.

Their father had died the winter before, crushed under a fallen ice shelf while hunting seals along the coast. The tribe had shrunk every season since. The yews near their camp, once plentiful, had been stripped too often, too deeply. The Fire Root was almost gone.

No more skins. No more tea.

Only hunger, cold, and memory.

That night, the brothers argued and then agreed. Both would take a supply of the tea skins and seeds from the remaining trees. They wrapped them in seal skin. To them, they were the most valuable of their possessions.

Viktor would go west; toward the Urals, toward the old Russian forests, toward what remained of the tribe's stories.

Arven would go east; toward the land bridge, toward ice and unknown shorelines.

Their mother lay between them, silent, as if guarding the choice.

By morning, Arven stood alone. Viktor had left with the sun at his back. The red skins were important, but not as important as fire. Arven noted that the fire in the hut had been disturbed by Viktor but he had left some for Arven.

The fire did not begin on the journey. It began in the hut, where it had burned longer than Arven could remember.

Arven stood alone in the half-light, listening to the fire settle into itself. Before dawn, he banked the fire pit and wrapped a single coal first in fungus and then soft bark. The coal remained burning and protected the way his mother had taught him and her mother before her.

The ember breathed slowly in his hands…not flame, but a promise.

## ARVEN'S JOURNEY — ACROSS BERINGIA

Arven left the hut and the life he had known. He crossed the frozen tundra hard as stone. Winds cut through the seams of his clothes and the seams froze shut with the freezing temperature. He ate dried reindeer meat until it was gone, then marrow scraped from old bones. Later, seal fat traded from coastal hunters.

He carried his fire as he walked, checking it often, feeding it carefully, never more than it needed. When the wind rose, he turned his body to shield it. When it dimmed, he knelt and coaxed it back, patient as stone.

Fire was not something you made. It was something you kept.

"At the top of a rise in the land he saw flat land with water on both sides, the bridge to another land. He could see other travelers walking to the far land. He ran and fell down many times until he the water separated by this stretch of land.

It was called Beringia, later known as the Bering Land Bridge to Alaska."

Arven sang as he walked, not in words, not yet.

It was a low humming cadence shaped by breath and footfall, rising and falling with the land. Part prayer, part instinct.

The sound carried no names, only direction: water downhill, sun behind the shoulder, stone before nightfall.

He did not think of it as memory. It was simply the way the body reminded itself to keep moving. The rhythm repeated in uneven cycles—never exact, but never lost—meant to survive forgetting.

The land bridge ended in a wall of ice.

The inland ice corridor that so many had mentioned would be available for his walk was closed. The walls of ice higher than cliffs shut off the inland route south. Arven stayed close to the water and turned south, following the coast.

He felled a tree with his only tool—a hand-shaped axe of stone, hafted with sinew and patience. He chose the tree carefully, listening to its weight, its balance, the way it answered the wind. When it fell, he thanked it, because taking without thanks had consequences even then.

For days he worked the wood. The axe opened the grain; shells from the shore refined it, scraping and smoothing where stone would split. He burned the heart slowly, feeding the fire like a thing alive, then cut again, shaping hollow from mass. There was no hurry. A canoe made in haste would betray you at sea.

He strengthened the hull with bone and seal sinew, stitched where the wood thinned, trusting tension more than thickness. The seams he sealed with pitch softened over fire and mixed with rendered fat, pressed deep until the wood drank it in. When the canoe touched water, it did not float so much as settle, finding its place.

He loaded little. A tool. A shell blade. Food enough to begin again. At first light, he pushed off and turned south, keeping the coast within reach, the land always near his shoulder.

He did not name the journey. He simply followed the water.

At night, he pulled the canoe above the tide line and crawled beneath it, wrapped in kelp and furs. When he had crab or fish, he sealed it in bull kelp with seal blubber, folding the leaves tight and binding them with sinew. The fat slowed rot. The kelp hid the scent.

Bull kelp tangled around the hull—thick, rubbery, smelling of salt and decay. It cut the wind and blurred his shape against the shore. When hunger came, he ate slowly, taking what the sea had already taught him how to keep.

Sometimes he paddled with others for a day or two. Sometimes he slept near their fires. But he always moved on alone.

The Fire Root seeds from the Siberian hut weighed little, so he carried them. Never letting them out of his sight.

## THE FORK

At a place where the coast bent inward, Arven met a woman.

She sat on a drift log near a small fire, mending a net with hands that moved without hurry. Furs wrapped her shoulders. Her hair was bound with sinew and shell. When she noticed him, she did not reach for her knife.

He lifted one hand and waited.

She nodded once and motioned him closer to the fire.

In silence, they shared fish roasted on stone. Later, as the tide withdrew, they slept wrapped together in seal skin and bear furs. She carried a stone knife sharpened thin as ice, used it to clean the fish he caught, and wiped it carefully before she slept.

She knew the inland routes. She knew the storms. She knew when to walk, and when not to.

They canoed south together along the coast, toward people, deer, and safety. But after two days of canoeing she indicated she want to turn toward the sunrise, toward a body of water so large Arven could not see the far shore.

He lifted his canoe. And followed.

## THE GREAT INLAND WATER

They portaged east over stone and ice, through valleys carved raw by floods that no longer ran. The land bore scars of water older than memory.

Then the lake appeared.

It was vast, cold, steel-blue, and endless. The far shore dissolved into sky. They paddled close to the lake edges, reading wind and cloud, sleeping at night on narrow stone beaches beneath overhanging rock. They ate fish when they could catch them, berries when they found them frozen and sweet beneath snow. When they killed a deer, they celebrated quietly, wrapping the meat in seal skin and ice to carry forward. Always protecting the fire embers.

Arven hummed the song his mother had taught him—a low sound, part breath, part rhythm. There were no words as he understood them, only direction: water, shelter, movement. Over time, he taught the woman the sound. She did not ask what it meant. She listened, then joined him.

Their voices aligned. They paddled as one.

But the lake took its toll.

Arven began to weaken. The inland cold settled deeper than coastal wind. His joints ached. His vision blurred in the mornings. He dreamed of his mother's hands, empty now, moving without purpose.

## THE STORM ON THE WATER

The storm came without warning.

Wind poured down from the high ridges, flattening the lake and then breaking it open. Waves rose fast, sharp and close together, slamming the canoe sideways. Rain followed, hard, cold, stinging like gravel.

The woman shouted once, just a sound, not a word, and turned them toward shore.

They did not reach the shore.

A wave lifted the canoe and dropped it again. Arven's grip slipped. For a moment the lake owned them.

The woman reached for the bundled bull kelp lashed behind the seat. She cut it loose and fed it over the bow, letting the heavy fronds drag in the water.

The canoe steadied immediately, its motion slowed, the bow pulled into the waves instead of sliding sideways.

Arven followed her movements without thinking, numb hands obeying knowledge older than fear.

They ran the canoe onto a narrow rock shelf as the storm broke fully. Wind searched for edges. Rain hammered stone.

They pulled the canoe high and turned it over. Together they layered bull kelp over hull and bodies, weaving fronds through lashings, pressing the slick leaves flat against the ground. The kelp bent. It did not tear. Water ran over them instead of beneath.

They lay curled together under the canoe, wrapped in furs and kelp, breathing salt and rot and rain. The smell hid them. The weight anchored them.

When hunger came, the woman unwrapped fish sealed in blubber and kelp. They ate slowly, sharing warmth, letting the fat settle heat into their chests.

By morning, the storm had passed.

The lake lay broken and white with foam. The kelp clung where they had placed it, torn in places, spent.

They gathered the fire embers and what could be used again and left the rest for the water.

Neither spoke.

## THE EASTERN SHORE

At the far eastern edge of the lake, the woman stopped.

The forest there was different. Old—not dense, but patient. The air held moisture without cold. Arven knelt and pressed his fingers into the soil. It was deep and dark and damp.

It felt like home.

Beneath towering trees, he found yews, slow, shadowed. Their needles glossy even in winter. Protected.

He looked at the woman. She nodded.

They would stop here.

Arven planted every aril he had carried from the land that had been. He pressed the soil flat with bare hands and hummed the song again this time softly, so the roots would hear it.

He never saw the trees grow.

## THE PEOPLE WHO KEPT THE ROOT

They stayed.

Over the centuries children came. His name became theirs. The chant survived—altered, shortened, hidden inside lullabies and work songs.

The yews grew slowly, as Arven had known they would. They took the skins from the existing yews to make tea and planted what they had brought. They learned that poison could guard life if boundaries were respected. They learned that taking too much killed everything.

Far away, his brother's line endured differently.

Two paths. One root.

The QWB screen went dark.

## AFTERMATH — NINTHWAVE HQ

The room was silent.

Caleb's hands trembled. "That melody," he said at last. "My grandfather used to hum it to me. I never knew why."

Danny swallowed. "My grandmother called us Whulshad. Said it meant *keepers*. I thought it was just a word."

On the screen, Q'ARIUM'S character of Arven's face—etched now with the lines of an old warrior, looked back at them.

The Whulshad name had crossed ice, flood, and time.

For a heartbeat, the room didn't breathe.

Danny and Caleb stared at the screen, then at each other like they were checking to make sure the other one was real, that the words hadn't rearranged themselves when they blinked. A laugh escaped Danny first, small and disbelieving, the kind that comes out when your body doesn't know whether to cry or grin. Caleb's shoulders lifted with a slow exhale, tension draining out of him in a way no one had realized he'd been carrying. Around them, their coworkers shifted closer, murmuring, the air suddenly bright with that shared, stunned happiness people get when a mystery finally clicks into place.

It wasn't just an answer. It was *their* answer.

They hadn't been chasing a ghost story after all. They hadn't imagined the pull, the strange familiarity, the sense that something old had been waiting for them to notice. The past wasn't distant anymore. It had reached forward and touched them on the shoulder.

"What matters," I said quietly, letting the moment have its breath before we moved on, "is that the Fire Root was carried here. Planted. Protected."

## *Conclusion*

The Scenario App completed its presentation of what it had found from its research into the yew tea. It had given us a look back into ancient history of the non poison use of the yew. It had also given Danny and Caleb a history.

The summit ended without discussion. Everyone left with the feeling that they were part of a story that was more than just developing a deep burn salve.

I wanted to talk to Skip about the full capability of the QWB so I asked Skip to stay on the QWB and to get P² on the line.

### Scene Four: Quantum Whisper Bridge Expansion
*Mammoth Lakes — TNIC Command Lab*

Skip brought P² onto the QWB channel. The secure icon pulsed once, then steadied.

P² appeared onscreen from the basement lab, the faint hum of the Q'Adler system behind him.

"Yeah, boss. What's up?"

Skip didn't waste time. "JP and I want a status check. We need to be certain the QWB meets Admiral Brewer's criteria for Pentagon-level secure communications."

P² smiled faintly. "It does. Anything transmitted within the cleared NinthWave team stays sealed. No bleed. No external visibility. You're clear to use it whenever you need."

"Good," Skip said. Then, carefully, "You once mentioned this was only the beginning of what QWB could become. Has that changed?"

P² leaned back slightly. "Funny you should ask."

I stayed quiet. When P² got that tone, it meant he'd already crossed the bridge and was waiting to see who followed.

"In real cloak-and-dagger work," he continued, "secure communication is only half the problem. The other half is memory, what gets said when one party isn't cleared."

I felt my shoulders tighten.

"Most people handle that with consent recordings or hardware bugs," P² said. "Both are detectable. Both leave trails. I've been working on something else, an extension of QWB that captures a conversation without transmitting anything and without alerting the other party."

Skip didn't react. Neither did I.

"It records without emission," P² added. "No signal. No RF. No software footprint. And it's governed under the same counterintelligence thresholds as QWB itself."

That mattered.

Skip finally spoke. "You're saying it can record a non-cleared conversation and preserve it for later analysis…quietly."

"Yes," P² said. "And once captured, it can't be altered."

I leaned forward. "That would be invaluable if Georg is meeting Russian executives under a commercial cover. Especially if we believe there's more going on than they're saying."

P² nodded. "Exactly."

Skip exhaled. "Show us."

The camera shifted. P² opened a matte-black case on the bench in front of him. Inside were three items, neatly arranged.

"This extension has three components," he said. "Simple. Closed loop."

He lifted the first.

"The polymer patch receiver. Thin. Flexible. Passive. It doesn't listen in the traditional sense, it captures quantum variance already present in the environment. No emissions, no probing. In our case, it sits inside a cufflink."

He glanced at the screen. "Activation is manual. A squeeze. No accidental capture."

He set it down and picked up the second item.

"The storage vial. This holds the captured whisper in suspension. Tamper-evident. Any attempt to open it without the paired quantum key collapses the state and destroys the data."

Skip murmured, "So interception equals loss."

"Always," P² said.

Finally, he gestured toward the system behind him.

"QWB itself. When the vial is docked, the whisper is decoded inside a controlled environment. No transmission ever crosses space. Everything stays contained."

Skip leaned closer to the screen. "So nothing broadcasts."

"Correct," P² said. "The Whisper holds its breath."

There was a pause.

"One rule," P² added. "Once captured, the record is immutable. No edits. No deletions."

Skip nodded slowly. "So are secrets."

"And truth," P² said quietly.

Outside the lab windows, first light touched the eastern Sierra. Granite peaks ignited in bands of cold gold while the valley below remained dark and still.

The system didn't announce itself. It waited.

# CHAPTER 16

# Stage 5 of the Discovery Protocol

**Scene One: The Day After the Summit**

Morning mist drifted across Padilla Bay in slow, silvery ribbons. The deck glistened with liquid sunshine, and Mandi and I sat in our rocking chairs, jackets zipped, coffee steaming between our hands. The house was quiet in a way that felt earned rather than empty.

The Summit still lingered with us: Q'ARIUM's reconstruction of Arven, the ancestral crossing, the planting of the first Fire Root grove. A myth rendered as pattern, not proof.

Now the team was dispersed. Each member working independently, but toward a shared objective spread across Seneca Ranch, Vienna, Bandai, Mammoth, and Texas. Each focused on a single task within Stage Five.

Stage Five was not about developing a therapy. It was about identifying, stress-testing, and discarding candidates until only those worth deeper pursuit remained.

I glanced at Mandi. "What do you think? Are we moving in the right direction?"

She took a measured sip of coffee. "Yes, but only if everyone stays tightly focused. We're closer than we've ever been, but we still don't understand the poison, its propagation, or its real clinical fit."

She paused. "Walk me through the encapsulation again."

"We isolate the active alkaloid, whatever it proves to be," I said. "Then encapsulate it so the shell dissolves only in damaged tissue. The compound activates locally, suppresses necrotic progression, and forms a biochemical barrier to halt spread."

"And Bandai's work?" she asked.

"DNA bombardment teaches recognition, pattern awareness without immune activation. DMSO provides penetration through the dermal layers."

She nodded. "Encapsulation, bombardment, transport. A disruptive architecture, if the molecule deserves it."

"That's the test," I said. "Stage Five is about finding something worthy of that architecture."

## Scene Two: Seneca Ranch, Big Timber, Montana — A Signal in the Noise

Seneca Ranch sat a few miles outside Big Timber, where land outlasted attention and privacy came naturally. To most, it was still a working sanctuary to save draft horses from slaughter- fences, barns, and long pasture lines running toward the foothills.

What few ever noticed was the secondary structure over the Boulder River from the main house: a purpose-built research alkaloid laboratory, established earlier during a different NinthWave venture, and kept operational precisely because it asked questions most institutions weren't ready to hear.

Sunlight cut through the high windows of the Seneca Alkaloid Laboratory, turning glassware amber. Chromatography pumps hummed softly.

Cam Williamson leaned over the monitor as a narrow peak rose-clean, repeatable.

"Run twenty-four," he recorded. "Fraction isolated from inner root sheath. Modified solvent sequence. Lower pH."

He ran the test again.

The peak returned.

"You're not paclitaxel," he murmured. "And you're not docetaxel."

The archive returned a single, neglected entry:

Unclassified diterpenoid fraction — Tag B-14 Unstudied. Unevaluated. Dormant.

Cam exhaled slowly. "Alright, B-14. Let's see who you are."

He didn't celebrate. Early signals failed more often than they survived.

He tapped one of his QWB nodes. I answered.

**Scene Three: QWB Link — Anacortes / Seneca Ranch**

"Cam," I said, as his lab came into view, "what have you got?"

"JP, you'll want to see this. Not a breakthrough, just something that refuses to disappear."

He rotated a small vial. "An interface compound. Trace alkaloid expression detected during aril–root boundary analysis. Low oxidation, stable under mild stress. In tissue assays, it shows differential behavior."

"Define differential."

"It responds weakly to necrotic markers," he said. "Signal detection, not selectivity. Not actionable yet."

I studied the spectrum. "It's smaller than the taxanes."

"More flexible," he agreed. "Likely a secondary metabolite. Could be adaptive or irrelevant."

"For now, it's a curiosity," I said.

"I'm calling it Bulbidraxine™ internally," Cam added. "Placeholder only."

"Send a micro-sample to Bandai," I said. "Low-energy testing only. No assumptions."

Bandai Pharmaceutical's advanced research laboratories were located roughly one hundred seventy-five miles north of Tokyo, in Fukushima Prefecture, high in the Bandai-Asahi mountain region. The site had been chosen decades earlier for its isolation, seismic stability, and cold-climate consistency. Conditions ideal for low-energy biochemical observation. Where most modern labs were built for speed, Bandai had been built for patience.

### Scene Four: Bandai Laboratories — Early Sparks

Under white lab lights, Kenji Nacheda-san examined the vial with care.

"Kirei da," he murmured.

He activated the QWB console. My image resolved. Nacheda-san was connected to me in Anacortes.

"Testing has begun," Nacheda-san said. "Observation-only bombardment. No genetic shaping."

"Good," I replied. "We're watching, not steering."

Gentle ionic pulses passed through the compound. Under magnification, Bulbidraxine™ flickered—not degradation, not activation, simply response.

"It does not collapse," Nacheda-san said. "That alone matters."

"But it doesn't penetrate deeply," I said.

"No. Surface response only. Clinically insufficient."

"Then it's not a therapy."

"Not yet," he agreed. "But it has internal coherence. That is uncommon."

"Continue carefully," I said. "Let the molecule tell us who it is."

"Hai," Kenji replied. "Nature first."

## Scene Five: Anacortes — The Realization

Night settled over Padilla Bay, fog soft against the windows. I sat at my desk as the QWB console blinked green—transmission complete.

Mandi entered with two mugs of tea. "Bandai?"

"Nacheda-san says the compound is stable," I said. "But he says it is too early. Too shallow to matter clinically."

"So not the barrier."

"No," I said. "But it's a thread. Not a solution."

She smiled. "Then Stage Five is working."

I closed my notebook gently.

"We didn't find the answer," I said. "But we found something worth studying."

Stage Five, was in progress.

# CHAPTER 17

# Train to Yekaterinburg, Russia

**Scene One: Andromeda Tower, Vienna**

Georg Messinger had spent three days replaying the Summit in his mind. NinthWave's progress impressed him, even if half the vocabulary still felt like alchemical poetry: alkaloids, encapsulation, DMSO vectors, DNA bombardment. He trusted JP and the others to understand it. His task lay elsewhere.

Now he had to discover whether the whispered rumors about TazNiva were true.

He reread Viktor Baranov's letter. The Q'ARIUM reconstruction of the Whulshad lineage had resurrected an ancient path with unsettling clarity. If Viktor's operation truly involved a tea derived from arils similar to those Arven once carried, then the past wasn't distant—it was active.

"It has to be the tea," Georg said aloud.

He tapped the QWB console. "Skip, I need a full intelligence profile on Viktor Baranov—past, present, everything. There is a side note as there was a coincidence with both the brother that went west and the TazNiva Biologics CEO."

"I caught that coincidence myself but it can't mean anything today Georg. It was thousands of years ago." He paused, "I am on your request," Skip replied. "Stand by."

Minutes later, a classified document appeared.

*John F. Derr, RPh, FASCP, FHIMSS*

## QWB / Q'ARIUM INTELLIGENCE PROFILE
**SUBJECT:** Viktor Sergeyevich Baranov
**CLASSIFICATION:** TOP SECRET — AUTHORIZED VIEW ONLY

**Born:** 1969, Nizhny Tagil, USSR
**Education:** Biochemical Engineering; State Institute of Chemical Technology, Moscow
**Postgraduate:** Academy of State Security — industrial counter-intelligence track (1994)

**Career Summary:**
- Analyst — Ministry of Natural Resources (biological patent monitoring)
- Deputy Director — Sverdlovsk-17 Research Complex (classified bioweapons decontamination)
- Founder/CEO — TazNiva Biologics (2005–Present)

**Aliases:** "The Engineer"

**Personality Profile (AI synthesis):**
Analytical: 93%
Empathic: 19%
Coercive: 68%
Adaptive: 47%

**Hidden-agenda probability:** 81% (High)

**Summary:** Operates under civilian façade; effectively aligned with Russia's strategic biosciences network. Cooperation with Aretē likely transactional and embedded in long-standing state monitoring rather than reactive intelligence.

What followed was a computer generated photograph of Viktor.

**Warning:** Do not discuss yew-derived compounds or Pentagon parameters during visit.

## *END OF REPORT*

Georg lowered the tablet and stared out over the Danube. *What have I walked into?*

There was purpose behind Viktor's smile. 'Control'.

He called to Klara. "Post a public announcement about my visit. Emphasize transparency and scientific collaboration."

"Yes, Dr. Messinger."

When the announcement went live, Georg whispered to himself, "An interesting trip indeed… and I intend to come back."

### Scene Two: Yekaterinburg: Viktor's Warning

In his office overlooking the facility rooflines, Viktor Sergeyevich Baranov reread his correspondence with Georg. Pleasant, professional, innocuous… too innocuous.

The teletype alarm chimed.

### GRU / Scientific Directorate — Priority Transmission
Monitoring alert based on ongoing interagency surveillance.
U.S. Embassy reports repeated Pentagon visits by Dr. Emily (DoD) and Dr. Jean Paul Kornig (NinthWave). Possible connection to Messinger's trip to TazNiva. Copies distributed to Scientific Security Registry.

Viktor folded the paper slowly.

"So," he murmured, "our Austrian guest arrives with American shadows at his back."

He turned to the window, watching steam drift from the vents of Sverdlovsk-17.

*Messinger is a polite man,* he thought. *Polite men often carry other people's questions.*

## Scene Three: Train to the Urals: Moscow–Yekaterinburg Express

The Moscow station echoed with metallic announcements and rolling luggage. Georg boarded the Trans-Ural Express—carriage polished, compartment small, window wide enough to frame a continent.

He logged into his QWB secure node.

Skip's overnight file: *Sverdlovsk-17 — Site Intel Overview.* Satellite images. Defense-linked shipping. Rosters of ex-military chemists and biodefense technicians.

"So, Viktor," Georg muttered, "your research may be natural, but your secrecy isn't."

The train moved through birch forests, white against shadowed pines. At each stop, the same man appeared—a gray coat, wire-rim glasses. Always present. Never engaged.

Georg noted him without reaction.

On the second night, with frost feathering the glass, Georg softly dictated into his QWB interface, triggering a passive whisper capture.

"Day Two. Possible surveillance on board—non-aggressive. Reviewing staff affiliations. Arrival expected at 9:00 AM local time."

The train rattled on.

Somewhere ahead lay Sverdlovsk-17, and a man who already knew he was coming.

## Scene Four: Viktor Prepares the Stage

Sverdlovsk-17 rose like a fortress between pines. Viktor paced the upper corridor, checking security feeds.

"Escort route: the analytical wing, purification, pilot hall," he told his aide. "No deviations."

He rehearsed the greeting smile in a reception mirror. Warm enough to seem human, empty enough to reveal nothing.

"Messinger," he said quietly, "let us see what you choose to notice."

## Scene Five: Arrival and Plant Tour

Snow drifted in thin flakes as Georg arrived at the compound. Viktor welcomed him at the steps.

"Dr. Messinger. Welcome to Sverdlovsk-17."

"Thank you. Russia still knows how to inspire awe."

"Space," Viktor replied, "is our most abundant resource."

Inside, the tour was efficient and curated. Extraction suites. Chromatography labs. Soviet legacy equipment alongside modern systems.

"We keep them for redundancy," Viktor said. "Old tools rarely fail."

"Neither, I suspect, do you," Georg replied.

Viktor's smile flickered, acknowledgment without confession.

## Scene Six: The Grove and the Truth

Plant manager Sergei Antonov drove Georg east to the greenhouse complex. Beyond the glowing glass structures, darker yew trunks threaded the forest.

"Russian Yew," Sergei said. "Old friend of this soil."

Inside, seedlings thrived in nutrient mist. Sergei hesitated, eyes shifting toward the main plant.

"The cancer line is real," he said finally. "But not the whole story."

Georg waited, then squeezed his cufflink lightly. A faint vibration. QWB recording was active.

"The most important product, the one the Generals care about, is made in a restricted wing. We call it the poison room."

"In the main facility?" Georg asked.

Sergei nodded once. "Tea from the arils. Low-dose, processed. Unofficially…" He said to himself, "Poison that feels like strength. That is the most dangerous kind."

## Scene Seven: The Urals: A Day Between Worlds

The next morning, Georg was driven east, away from the city and into the foothills of the Urals.

The driver introduced himself as Ivan. A man of few words, thick hands on the wheel, eyes that never lingered in mirrors longer than necessary. The car moved steadily along a narrowing road, asphalt giving way to patched concrete, then to frost-rimed gravel.

Birch forests lined the route, white trunks scarred with old burns. Beyond them rose darker stands of pine and fir, dense enough to swallow sound. Villages appeared without warning. Low houses hunched against the cold, roofs weighted with stones, smoke rising straight into a colorless sky. Old men watched from benches. Dogs that did not bark.

"These are the Iron Mountains," Ivan said at last, not looking at him. "Everything begins here. Rivers. Stories. People." He paused. "Endurance, especially."

The car climbed to a turnout above a river slicing through slate and iron-rich stone. The water ran fast and dark, meltwater cold enough to kill in minutes.

Georg stepped out. The air cut cleanly through his coat.

Beautiful, he thought, but not kindly.

As he looked across the valley, something stirred at the edge of his mind. This terrain is older than borders, older than nations, matched the migration models Skip had shown them at the summit. If a man had fled Siberia west instead of east… if he had carried seeds…

This would be the place.

A corridor. A pause between worlds.

"Scientists came here once," Ivan said quietly, standing beside him now. "During the old years. Some were invited."

The wind moved through the trees before he continued.

"Some stayed. Some did not."

Georg nodded, hands in his pockets. He did not ask which kind Ivan meant.

The wind moved through the trees like a low breath. Even the stones, Georg thought, remembered who passed through, and what they carried.

**Scene Eight: Farewell Dinner at the Dacha**

Viktor's dacha stood beyond the last village, tucked against the forest where the trees pressed close, as if listening.

The house was old timber and stone, built to survive winters and regimes alike. One road led in. Georg noted, without comment, that there were no visible paths leading out.

Warm light glowed through thick windows but did not travel far.

Elena Baranova greeted him at the door. Her welcome was courteous, precise. She wore no jewelry, no excess. Her eyes missed nothing.

"Dinner is ready," she said. "You've been in the mountains?"

"Yes," Georg replied. "They have a long memory."

Elena inclined her head slightly. "So do people who live among them."

The meal was heavy and deliberate: dark bread, venison, pickled roots, a clear spirit poured without ceremony. No music. Only the fire, and the quiet discipline of conversation held in check.

Midway through dinner, Viktor set down his glass.

"I hear Aretē may shift Taxol production to the United States," he said casually, as if discussing weather patterns.

"A possibility," Georg replied. "Efficiency."

"Efficiency," Viktor echoed, turning the word slowly. "A polite way to describe surrendering control."

Georg met his gaze. "Even a soul," he said evenly, "needs light to survive."

The fire snapped sharply.

Viktor smiled thinly. "You Europeans still believe stories shape the world."

"Stories carry people," Georg replied. "Sometimes seeds as well."

Viktor waved a hand. "Folklore. Migration myths. Every forest claims to be the beginning of something."

Elena refilled Georg's glass, not looking at Viktor as she did so.

"Some beginnings," she said softly, "leave traces."

Silence settled again.

Outside, the forest creaked as temperatures dropped. Somewhere beyond the tree line, a dog howled once, then stopped. Georg noticed that the windows reflected the room more than the dark beyond them.

He ate carefully. Spoke little. Observed everything.

This was not a place to argue truth.

It was a place to remember it.

**Scene Nine: Afterward**

The next day, Viktor summoned Sergei.

"You mentioned nothing unnecessary?" Viktor asked.

"No, sir."

"A careless word becomes treason," Viktor said coldly. "And treason freezes quickly."

Sergei nodded, pale.

When he left, Elena whispered, "You frightened him."

"Good," Viktor replied. "Cold preserves obedience."

**Scene Ten: Flight to Vienna: Whisper in Transit**

High above the Russia, Georg touched his cufflink.

"JP, dual production confirmed. Public cancer derivative; hidden military tonic derived from arils. Endurance enhancer. Subtle. Controlled."

Pause.

"Possibly worse."

Two taps. Whisper sealed.

Back in Andromeda Tower, Georg finished his notes and closed the secure file.

Dual lines. Poison room. Military interest in Fire Root tea.

He did not write more. He didn't need to.

Georg moved to the window. Below him, the Danube slid eastward, carrying the city's lights into the dark. Vienna always looked calm from above—ordered, symmetrical, civilized. Empires had trusted that illusion before. So had physicians.

He thought of the Vienna clinics he'd trained in, the old lecture halls where medicine had once promised liberation through understanding. This city had built an identity out of diagnosis, out of naming what others refused to name. Freud's Vienna had believed truth could heal, that if you dragged the hidden thing into the light, it would loosen its grip.

But Vienna had also been a city of protocols and quiet authority. White coats. Closed doors. Consent implied rather than spoken. In the archives and museums, the past still clung to the instruments: the neatness of the tools, the confidence of the hands that held them. Other eras had believed discipline could cure what compassion could not.

Both had been certain they were right.

Georg rested his palm against the glass. Chemistry, he knew, was never moral. It obeyed structure, not intention. The same compound could numb pain or sharpen obedience. The difference was never in the molecule. It was in the hand that deployed it, and the boundary that hand refused to cross.

In the Urals, those boundaries had felt... flexible.

He exhaled slowly.

Every cure has a mirror image, he thought. And every civilization decides which one it is willing to see.

Outside, Vienna's lights shimmered across the river—beautiful, controlled, enduring. Georg turned from the window and dimmed the room, leaving only the glow of the city reflected faintly in the glass.

Some discoveries, he knew, were meant to be slowed.

And some stories, no matter how old, were not meant to be repeated.

# CHAPTER 18

# Russia

**Scene One: Sverdlovsk-17 — Institute for Natural Products Research**

Monday morning came sharp and cold, the kind of light that made the Urals look carved from iron. In his office at Sverdlovsk-17, Viktor Sergeyevich Baranov sat before the double-paned window, watching snow clouds creep low across the mountains. His report to Moscow waited on his desk. One of those deceptively simple updates that demanded absolute care.

It had to be brief. Reassuring. Empty of anything that could grow teeth.

In Russia, a single paragraph could become a novel once passed through enough ministries. Everyone added interpretation. Everyone added suspicion. By the time a report reached its final destination, the original meaning was usually unrecognizable.

And this time, truth was dangerous.

Dr. Georg Messinger's visit had been polite, formal, and entirely too perceptive. Two seasoned scientists pretending not to watch each other, while watching everything.

What Moscow must not learn was the full truth about Zar-Chai tea, the yew-aril stimulant. And certainly not that Messinger's questions had wandered too close to it.

"His visit has to be about the tea not the cancer drug," Viktor said aloud.

He pressed the black telephone button.

"Doctor Petrova. My office. Now."

Within minutes, Dr. Irina Petrova, Chief of Clinical Operations, stood before him.

He gestured for her to sit.

"Doctor," Viktor said, making a steeple with his fingers, "explain everything about the tea: the process, the effects, the risks."

"Yes, Director," Irina Petrova replied.

She opened her notebook, graphite smudged along the margins.

"The material is derived from *Taxus borealis*. We harvest the berries when the aril that protects the seed, turns red. Next, remove the seed, and roast the shell of aril, until the outer coat splits. The thin brown skin, the testa, is peeled and ground. That layer contains a complex of alkaloids we classify as beta-taxenopyrine."

Viktor listened without interruption.

"We ferment the flakes for seventy-two hours with culture K-21. Acid cleavage converts part of the molecule into beta-taxenidine, a more active variant. After filtration and steeping, we obtain the white powder concentrate the soldiers call Zar-Chai."

"And the effects?" Viktor asked.

"Initial response in fifteen minutes: elevated heart rate, heightened visual acuity, reduced pain from cold or injury. Endurance nearly doubles."

"And long term?"

She hesitated.

"In the first year, excellent resilience. By years three to five, shortened sleep cycles, emotional flattening, tremor, dissociation. Neurological decline follows. We call it Zar Syndrome. We insist it doesn't exist."

Viktor exhaled slowly.

"So the miracle lasts long enough to break a warriors mind."

"Enough time to build an army," Irina replied.

He turned back to the window. Snow erased the mountains entirely.

"Prepare a summary for the Bureau," he said at last. "Use the endurance data. Omit the deterioration curve."

"Yes, Director."

At the door she paused. "If the Americans discover this, it will be a problem."

### *MOSCOW REPORT*

Alone again, Viktor typed:

**Subject:** Visit of Dr. G. Messinger — Summary Findings

- **Observation:** Routine inspection. No competitive intelligence indicated.
- **Plant Status:** Operations normal.
- **Supplement Program:** Within expected parameters.
- **Endurance Index:** +31%.
- **Recommendation:** Continue production at current levels.

He saved the file. The red indicator light blinked waiting to transmit.

In Moscow, the message would arrive before dawn. Someone would read it twice. Someone would quietly mark the file for follow-up.

Viktor hit the transmit key.

Viktor shut down his terminal and stepped into the snow, carrying the silence of Sverdlovsk-17 like a second coat.

# CHAPTER 19

# Reports and Counterplots

**Scene One: Georg's Debrief to NinthWave Biobotanica**

Mandi and I were seated at the NinthWave Biobotanica headquarters boardroom table in Anacortes when I opened the QWB secure channel to Skip Howard at TNIC in Mammoth Lakes, California.

Morning fog off Padilla Bay drifted against the glass wall behind Mandi, soft gray ribbons blurring the shoreline below. The steady hum of the conference unit filled the silence as the encryption lights pulsed amber.

"Skip, Georg has completed his visit to Sverdlovsk-17 and is ready to debrief us," Mandi said.

Skip's voice came through immediately. "I already pulled the metadata. Georg used his QWB cufflink extensively while on site. I recommend we listen to the audio feed first so we're aligned."

For the next few minutes, we ran the compressed recording at double speed. Viktor Baranov's voice, echoes of factory floors, and fragments of Russian conversation drifted in and out. When the playback ended, we patched in Georg's Vienna office.

After brief greetings, Georg began.

"I had a shadow the entire trip, visible enough to be intentional. He didn't interfere, only made sure I understood I wasn't alone."

"The time at the plant was formal. They demonstrated bark harvesting and processing into Toxan™, their oncology compound. Viktor understood why I was there, and I understood that he understood. Polite tension. Gamesmanship, but restrained."

"There was one sealed room I wasn't permitted to enter. They claimed it housed high-toxicity work on the yew's poisonous fractions. My escort was explicit about keeping clear."

"My escort wasn't Viktor. It was Colonel Sergei Antonov, the military liaison—polite, measured, eyes never smiling. On Saturday he took me to the yew groves. They're using the entire tree, not just the bark. I didn't ask about growth cycles, but I'm confident they're working with a faster-maturing strain than the Pacific Yew. I also believe they're isolating a different alkaloid."

"Our conversations kept circling supply, Russia's shipments to us in Vienna. They know Aretē could cancel the contract at any time, but no one said it aloud."

"Finally, almost casually, Antonov mentioned a military contract. Something about a tea. He called it a morale aid for soldiers. No elaboration. But it lingered."

I said, "That mention pushes this beyond research. We should bring the Admiral into this immediately."

"Agreed," Skip said.

"I think it's time for an in-person session with the Admiral's group," I added.

"Agreed," Mandi said.

"Georg," I asked, "anything else that is urgent?"

"No," Georg replied. "New information to watch, but as you Destroyer-men used to say, steaming as before. Watch your mirrors."

The line went dead. Skip signed off moments later.

Mandi and I sat quietly.

"When we started," she said, "this was a two-foot-square puzzle. By week eight, it should have been smaller. Instead, it's grown."

"We're narrowing chemistry," I said, "but widening consequences."

She nodded. "A meeting with the Admiral, Emily, and Hank McKenna is the right move."

I called the Admiral. He listened, then scheduled an in-person meeting for the following Monday.

"Seven days," I said after ending the call.

She smiled faintly. "We'll be ready."

## Scene Two: Directive Echo — Tea

In a ten-by-ten room beneath the Kremlin's military wing, Corporal Yuri Krylov sat alone at his desk. The air smelled faintly of ozone and floor wax. A single bulb lit the tabletop; the rest of the room stayed in shadow.

Yuri was rereading a battered, censored copy of Clancy's *The Hunt for Red October*. In this version, the Russian hero was Captain Alexei Borodin of the K-412 *Red Dawn*. The final line—*Now what?* always made Yuri smile.

In the original book, before the redactions, before the substitutions, the Americans had understood something important: that systems broke not from rebellion, but from friction. Yuri had read an imported copy once, years ago, before it vanished from the library. He remembered thinking it was indulgent. Too romantic. Too Western in its need for heroes.

This version was better. Cleaner. Safer.

In this edition, Captain Borodin did not defect. He tested the Americans instead. He returned to his Russian port. Order was preserved. The system worked.

Yuri preferred that ending.

Real life did not allow for lone captains making moral decisions. Real life ran on memos, stamps, and routing protocols. Real life advanced because everyone performed their assigned role and trusted the layers above them to see what they could not.

That was why the margin notes amused him. Чушь! Nonsense. The idea that one man could slip through an empire and change the balance of power.

Empires did not fall because of books. They shifted because of terminology.

Tea.

He frowned briefly at the word, then dismissed the thought. Linguistic coincidence was a known hazard of translation. Analysts were trained not to anthropomorphize patterns.

He closed the book, squared the cables, and returned them to their folders.

Order restored.

On his shelf sat a message received three days earlier, shortly after the Americans' first in-person defense-health meeting. Routine. Harmless.

**To:** U.S.A. Observation Activity Directorate, Kremlin Military HQ
**From:** U.S. Embassy, Washington, D.C. **Subj:** Quarterly Update

Digital observation of the Pentagon reveals a meeting between Assistant Secretary of Defense for Health Affairs Admiral Albert Brewer, USN; General Hank McKenna; Dr. Emily Vargas, a burn and reconstructive specialist with a primary appointment at the University of Texas Houston Burn and Reconstruction Center and a joint affiliate role at Memorial Hermann's John S. Dunn Burn Center; and Dr. **Jean Paul Kornig**, President of NinthWave Biobotanica, Inc. Subject unknown. AI profiling suggests topical burn care. Military enhancement ("tea") not a subject.

**Conclusion — Not an issue.**

Yuri had stamped it **FOR INFORMATION** and forwarded it to Corporal Anya Morozova at the Military Morale Directorate. Then he'd forgotten it.

The teletype erupted again.

**From:** Viktor Baranov, Director, Institute for Natural Products Research (Sverdlovsk-17) **Ref:** Kremlin Military Contract No. 741 — Military (Tea)

Visit by President of Vienna-based DPC Division of Aretē Pharmaceutical Company. No reference to alternative products supplied to the Russian Military ("Tea").

**Conclusion — Non-issue.**

Yuri stared.

Tea.

Same word. Same denial.

That was never coincidence.

He laid the two messages side by side, re-stamped them, and added a short note:

> ***Forwarded for Information — Possible***
> ***terminology cross-reference ("Tea").***

He sent the bundle up the pneumatic tube.

From there, it moved quickly—office manager to section chief, section chief to Foreign Intelligence Center. By evening, both cables were stamped **URGENT** and rerouted to the Kremlin's Top-Secret Tea Project directorate.

Analysts compared Baranov's sanitized report with the Embassy cable.

Their conclusion: the Americans may already know about the Tea enhancement.

Directives went out to monitor all U.S. scientific contacts linked to NinthWave or Aretē.

At the Russian Embassy in Washington, a senior attaché read the order and transmitted a single encrypted line to a dormant field operative in Houston:

***Acquire verification of Dr. Emily Vargas's research. No casualties.***

Back in his basement office, Yuri Krylov knew none of this. He finished *Red October*, smiled at the margin scrawl—Чушь! (Nonsense.) and added his own 'nonsense' beside it.

Outside his door, the pneumatic tube hissed again, carrying his "non-issue" upward through the Kremlin like a signal climbing into the wires.

# CHAPTER 20

# Pentagon Briefing and Houston Incident

**Scene One: Pentagon Briefing and Houston Incident**

The secure conference room in the Office of the Assistant Secretary of Defense for Health Affairs was silent except for the faint hum of air circulation.

Present were the four original members of the team: Admiral Albert Brewer, General Hank McKenna, Dr. Emily Vargas, and me.

It had been just over two months since the project began. Barely enough time to define a chemistry pathway, but long enough to feel the weight behind it. The room's status lights glowed red, signaling full isolation from the Pentagon network.

Admiral Brewer began, voice low and deliberate. "I hope everyone's holding up. It's been two months since our last in-person. I've seen fragments of information, but I want a clear sense of where we are. JP, start us off."

"Admiral," I said, "a great deal has been done. We're refining the compound structure, and Emily can confirm the clinical target and assay endpoints are locked. But we're not ready for the full, comprehensive status report yet."

Brewer's eyes narrowed slightly. "Why not?"

"Because we're entering the final proof phase," I said. "Stage Five accelerated after the aril breakthrough. Within ten days, the Monday after next, we expect to have the lead compound identified, the mechanism mapped against the deep-burn pathway, and a prototype salve prepared for controlled evaluation. That briefing will be our milestone."

Brewer held my gaze for a beat, then nodded once. "All right. Ten days. I'll schedule it."

I continued. "In the meantime, there's a separate matter. One that belongs as much in Hank's world as mine."

McKenna leaned forward. "Go ahead."

"In the course of verifying our yew-derived production line," I said, "we've come across credible indications of a Russian-issued endurance aid. Some form of fermented tea or extract, possibly derived from related botanical material. Crude, but reportedly effective."

Brewer glanced at McKenna. "General?"

McKenna nodded. "Bits and pieces. Our intel people think their medical corps is issuing something mixed in water before operations. Mild for routine units, likely stronger variants for specialty elements. Similar chatter shows up along the Belarusian border and in North Korea. Same thread, different packaging."

"Exactly," I said. "Our concern is not the substance itself, it's the interpretation. If they think we're building a stimulant, we become a counterintelligence target. Perception can become intelligence faster than we can correct it."

Brewer's expression hardened. "Is there any direct connection to our work?"

"No, sir," I said. "The chemistry may rhyme, but the intent does not. Still, if we can verify what they're using, we get a defensive edge. We understand what they're feeding their troops, and we avoid being misread as chasing the same objective."

Dr. Vargas spoke for the first time, controlled and clinical. "If you can obtain even an anecdotal sample, anything analyzed safely, I'd like to see whether there's structural overlap with what we're building for burn containment. Not for military enhancement. For toxicity and mechanism."

Brewer nodded. "Approved. Stay focused. We're in the healing business, not the hurting one."

He gathered his folder. "JP, your compound briefing is confirmed for the Monday after next. Hank, handle counterintelligence off-line unless it intersects directly with this project. Emily, coordinate through Health Affairs channels only. Dismissed."

"Aye, Admiral," McKenna said.

"Yes, sir," Vargas replied.

I stood. "Understood."

As the door sealed behind us, I felt it an invisible shift in the venture. The science hadn't changed. The weather around the science had.

### *Two Days Later — Houston, Texas*

It was a mild Saturday evening when Dr. Emily Vargas left the Texas Medical Center Biotherapeutics Lab. Her briefcase was heavy with conference notes, burn-care drafts, and contact patterns from the week. Nothing classified, but enough to confirm who was speaking to whom and how often.

The parking lot was nearly empty.

As she reached for her car door, the passenger door of the adjacent sedan swung open, cutting off her path. A man stepped out—well-dressed, middle-aged, controlled—moving with the calm of someone used to compliance.

Emily froze.

He didn't raise his voice. He didn't display a weapon. He simply closed the distance and took her arm with firm certainty, just enough to make resistance feel pointless.

"Please," he said in lightly accented English, "don't shout. I'm not going to hurt you."

"What do you want?" she managed.

"Your briefcase."

The words were rehearsed, delivered like a lab protocol.

Before she could find her voice again, he took the case and guided her into her vehicle with a hand at her elbow—not intimate, not violent, just practiced. Then he was gone, his sedan rolling out into Houston traffic as if nothing had happened.

Emily sat motionless for two heartbeats, then pulled her phone with shaking hands.

"Hank, it's Emily. Someone just took my briefcase."

McKenna's voice was immediate. "Are you injured?"

"No. Just shaken."

"Stay where you are. I'm getting someone to you. Now."

## The Next Morning — Pentagon QWB Link

We reconvened by secure video. Brewer's expression was grim. McKenna looked carved from stone. Dr. Vargas was composed, but I could see the fatigue at the edges. The kind that comes after a shock when your body refuses to admit it's been shocked.

McKenna spoke first. "No harm done. The briefcase was open literature, notes, and patterns—confirmation material. I believe the Russians wanted to verify we are not doing stimulant work. They have their answer."

Brewer nodded once, slow. "So they're watching, but still uncertain."

He turned his eyes toward me. "JP, tighten the security of your people. Keep communications disciplined. The optics have changed."

"Understood, Admiral," I said.

Brewer continued. "We stay on target. JP, ten days to the feasibility report and compound identification briefing. Hank, handle counterintelligence off-line unless it intersects the science. Emily, if you pursue analysis of any stimulant sample, it stays in the lane: toxicity, overlap, defense."

Dr. Vargas hesitated, then spoke softly. "Sir, if we can obtain a sample safely, I want to know what it does to tissue systems. If there's systemic toxicity, I want it flagged before anything goes near clinical trials."

Brewer's answer was immediate. "Approved. And keep your focus. We heal."

He looked into the camera. "Right, JP?"

"Aye, aye, Admiral," I said.

The screen went dark.

I sat in the quiet afterward, staring at my own reflection in the black glass. Two sciences, side by side. One meant to heal, one meant to control, and the distance between them shrinking whenever someone decided the ends justified the means.

We would not become that.

Not even by accident.

**Scene Two: Seneca Ranch Laboratory, Big Timber, Montana**

Winter sun lifted over Seneca Ranch and spilled through the high lab windows, turning glassware pale gold. Outside, across the Boulder River, the Sweet Grass pastures lay still under a thin crust of snow. In the far paddock, Promise, the Premarin colt with the faint blaze, trotted playful arcs around older mares, breath rising and fading in the cold air.

Inside, the lab moved with quiet purpose: pumps whispering, peristaltic tubing pulsing, centrifuges humming as pale-red liquid ran through glass columns.

Cam Williamson leaned over the console beside Peters, the technician assisting him. "Pressure steady?"

"Forty-one millibars and holding," Peters said, adjusting a valve. "Extract is clearing."

The liquid coiled down through the separator, luminous, like crimson glass diluted by light. Cam watched without blinking. "That's it," he said quietly. "B-24 fraction… Bulbidraxine precursor."

At the adjoining bench, Pinella recorded readings from the thermal scanner, eyes moving from screen to screen. "Spectral signature matches the earlier sample," she said. "Backbone stability holds."

Son of White Man Running (known to everyone at Seneca Ranch simply as Son, head of Ranch Operations), was already up before dawn, moving quietly among the horses and walking to the Lab.

He assisted Cam by moving between workstations, checking reactor temperatures. "This aril pulp is softer than anything we've run before," he said. "We'll need vacuum drying if you want pure crystallization."

Cam nodded. "Pre-vac at twenty Celsius. Keep it pliable enough to bond with the polymer before it hardens."

Mariah Haynes, the owner of Seneca Ranch and Mandi's sister, came in wearing her barn jacket, cold clinging to her sleeves. She looked at the screens and then at Cam. "You all sound like surgeons arguing over a heartbeat!"

Cam's mouth twitched. "We might be."

Pinella stepped aside so Mariah could see the shallow dish on the workstation: a delicate film glistening under the lamp. Sweet Water Grass™ polysaccharide refined into a stabilizing medium.

"This is your sweet grass at work," Pinella said. "Long polymer chains. They can wrap the alkaloid and keep it stable during transfer."

Mariah leaned closer. "It's beautiful."

Cam drew a few drops of purified extract into a pipette and released them onto the film. The reaction was gentle, just a faint hiss and a shimmer of color, red turning to rose-gold as the alkaloid merged with the polymer.

Peters watched the monitor. "Oxidation rate down twenty percent. Stabilization complete."

"Good," Pinella said. "That's our encapsulation layer."

Son set down the assay dish: simulated dermal tissue under controlled enzyme exposure. "Ready for the test?"

Cam nodded once. "Let's see if it defends."

They placed a small square of polymer film over the damaged skin section and started the timer.

Ten minutes: unchanged. Twenty minutes: the red halo of enzymatic spread contracted. Thirty minutes: the breakdown curve flattened.

Pinella's voice went hushed. "Cam… it stopped."

Cam stared at the monitor as if it might lie. "Timestamp it. Record everything. Duplicate it."

Mariah let out a slow breath. "You mean it's working."

"It's doing more than working," Pinella said. "It's containing."

Cam keyed the secure line. The NinthWave QWB channel opened with a soft tone. "This is Seneca Ranch," he said. "Bulbidraxine precursor

B-24 extracted from aril matrix. Polymer encapsulation complete using Sweet Water Grass™ polysaccharide. Initial in-vitro burn assay shows enzymatic suppression inside thirty minutes. Transmitting spectral and assay data to Bandai for integration prep."

Outside, Promise kicked through the snow, shaking his mane as if the world were simple.

Inside, the lab didn't celebrate. It documented.

Because proof, not hope, was the only currency that mattered now.

# CHAPTER 21

# Admiral's Phase One Briefing

**Scene One: The Briefing**

The Pentagon Group of four met in the secure office complex of the Office of the Assistant Secretary of Defense for Health Affairs on Level E. Over two months had passed since the project's launch—long enough for real answers to emerge, and short enough that mistakes could still be corrected.

This was the Phase One gate.

After the easy greetings of colleagues who had grown into friends, Admiral Brewer nodded once.

"JP, the floor is yours."

"Thank you, Admiral. Bottom line, we've reached clinical feasibility on a deep-burn salve candidate and its delivery architecture. The science is new, the mechanism is sound, and it meets the objectives Emily and Hank defined at our first meeting."

I paused, then continued.

"My proposal for today is simple. First, I'll present the findings in the scientific and legal language required for your approval to proceed. Second, I'll restate them in plain terms—how a physician would explain this to a patient. Finally, we'll address outliers, including the Russian tea issue, and align on timing, scope, and Phase Two funding."

Brewer glanced at the others. "Hank? Emily?"

Both nodded.

"Admiral," I continued, "the NinthWave network has completed Phase I—Discovery—of our internal three-phase process: Discovery, Development, and Demonstration.

"We have isolated a previously uncharacterized aril-derived alkaloid fraction from the Pacific Yew, provisionally designated SW-9A. This compound shows targeted regenerative activity in deep thermal injury.

"It was first characterized at Seneca Ranch and independently validated at Bandai Laboratories in Japan and at NinthWave headquarters in Anacortes."

I advanced the display.

"Our findings rest on three pillars.

**I. Cellular Communication and Regeneration** SW-9A does not behave as a cytotoxin. In controlled assays, it arrests necrotic progression and initiates granulation within twelve hours. It functions as a regulatory signal, informing damaged cells where to stop dying and where to begin rebuilding. Internally, we refer to this as the Root Connection principle.

**II. Precision Delivery** Bandai achieved localized delivery using DNA bombardment paired with a DMSO carrier. Penetration reaches the deepest burn layers without systemic circulation. Cellular uptake occurs within six minutes; full therapeutic release by twelve. The compound remains confined to the injury site.

**III. Ethical Source Control** Natural yield from Pacific Yew is limited. Our protocol caps harvest at twenty-five percent of sustainable annual yield. All scale-up will rely on cultivated groves or semi-synthetic replication under Department oversight."

I looked back to the others.

"Together, these findings complete Phase One: compound identification, delivery verification, sourcing controls, and legal readiness. We have moved from hypothesis to confirmed clinical feasibility."

### Plain-Language Explanation

"Here's how I'd explain this to a patient.

"The Deep Burn Salve comes from a compound found in the Pacific Yew tree. A tree that has long been part of modern medicine. What we're using is not the cancer drug, and it's not a modified version of it. It's a different fraction, drawn from a different part of the tree, with a completely different biological role.

"When applied to a deep burn, the salve goes directly into the damaged tissue. It doesn't travel through the bloodstream and doesn't affect the brain. It calms the burn at depth, stops the injury from spreading, clears dead cells, and helps healthy skin rebuild from the inside out.

"Most burn treatments work on the surface. This one works where the burn actually lives. Because it stays localized, pain is reduced, healing accelerates, and scarring and infection risk are significantly lower.

"In simple terms: it helps the body remember how to heal."

### Legal Transition

I handed the folders across the table.

"The proposed amendment authorizes Phase Two—Development— upon approval."

Emily read the text carefully.

"JP," she said, "you're confident in this?"

"Yes," I replied. "Confident enough to proceed. Careful enough to keep questioning."

Brewer nodded once. "You're approved to move forward. Funding will be released."

### Scene Two: Emily's Tea Report

Emily Vargas straightened slightly.

"For the record, I serve as a clinical advisor to the Pentagon. My primary appointment is with the University of Texas Houston Burn and Reconstruction Center, with a joint affiliate role at Memorial Hermann's John S. Dunn Burn Center."

She placed a sealed container on the table.

"This is Zar-Chai. A powdered preparation distributed through Russian military channels."

She summarized calmly.

"It is aril-derived. Same botanical family, crude processing. Short-term endurance enhancement, followed by neurological degradation. It is not a weapon, but it is not medicine."

Brewer's voice hardened.

"So they're pushing physiology past recovery."

"Yes, sir."

Hank McKenna folded his arms. "Which puts this squarely in my lane."

**Scene Three: NinthWave Status Call**

That night, I briefed the global team.

"Phase Two plan is approved. We need plans and budgets in two weeks. Phase Two duration: six months. Fifty controlled trials—no more, no less."

No objections.

"Also," I added, "Phase One bonuses will be issued internally. You earned them."

The screens went dark.

## Scene Four: Reflection and Celebration

At the Anacortes Brown Lantern Tavern, the mood was lighter than it had been in days.

The place smelled of old wood, fried onions, and spilled beer that no amount of scrubbing ever quite erased. Nautical and Sport Team flags hung from the rafters, faded photos of past sporting events lined the walls, and the low ceiling trapped laughter the way the harbor trapped fog. It was the kind of room where stories stayed told.

Chris and Shana sat closer than before—close enough that when the table shook with laughter, neither shifted away. Chris angled his body toward hers without thinking; Shana mirrored him just as unconsciously. When the bartender dropped off another round, Chris slid Shana's glass toward her before she reached for it. She nodded once in thanks, their eyes meeting for a beat longer than necessary.

Mandi noticed. So did I.

Outside, the night air had sharpened, salt-heavy and cold. As the group stepped onto the sidewalk, Chris shrugged out of his jacket and handed it to Shana without comment. She hesitated only a second before slipping it on, tucking her hands into the pockets as if they belonged there.

No declarations. No rush.

Just something beginning.

Later, back home, Mandi and I sank into the warmth of the deck jacuzzi, steam rising into the dark like breath finally released.

"Phase Two," she said softly.

"And something else," I replied, watching the vapor disappear into the night.

She smiled. "Yes. Something else too."

# CHAPTER 22

# Zar-chai and the Oslo Agreement

**Scene One: Telex Room, Kremlin Military HQ**

Corporal Yuri Krylov sat in his cramped office deep within the Kremlin when the old teletype machine clattered to life again.

"Another message," he muttered, rolling his chair closer.

He had not seen this much traffic in weeks. Activity around Zar-Chai was accelerating, and he felt a faint, professional unease. Patterns mattered more than content, and this pattern was tightening.

The narrow strip of paper crawled out:

**US–Russian Embassy Observation Report**
From: Embassy Washington, D.C.
To: U.S.A. Observation Activity Directorate, Kremlin Military HQ
Subject: Update – Pentagon Medical Personnel

As directed, Emily Vargas delayed by embassy staff. Her briefcase seized, contents imaged, archived, and destroyed after review for Zar-Chai-related documents.

All papers were scientific analyses of topical burn ointments and salves. No references to Zar-Chai or soldier enhancement.

Today Dr. Jean Paul Kornig again met with Admiral Albert Brewer, General Hank McKenna, and Dr. Vargas for one hour under Top Secret cover. No intelligence gained on meeting content.

Embassy analysis: Group appears focused on evaluation of topical burn treatments using Kornig's plant expertise. No evidence of enhancement connection. Observation continues.

Yuri frowned.

The message read as harmless. Routine. Reassuring. Too reassuring.

Still, interpretation was not his role. Movement was.

He stamped the page and routed it upward.

To: General Aleksei Sokolov, Officer in Charge U.S.A. Observation Activity Directorate, Kremlin Military HQ

"My job is just to pass the paper," Yuri reminded himself.

## Scene Two: Office of General Aleksei Sokolov

General Aleksei Sokolov leaned back in his worn leather chair and read the embassy telex twice.

As Viktor Baranov's direct military overseer, and final authority on compliance for all enhancement-adjacent programs, Sokolov rarely involved himself in factory level operations. When he did, it was never accidental.

Until now, he had treated Viktor's "magic tea" as a minor endurance aid. Zar-Chai had circulated quietly among Russian and North Korean units for years. Short deployments. Few complaints.

His real concern had always been the Koreans. No one knew what they fed their troops.

"What the hell," he muttered, "every North Korean life lost is a Russian life spared."

But this volume of embassy traffic bothered him.

Quiet relationships were meant to stay quiet. Noise was dangerous.

He opened a thin blue folder from his cabinet:

**THE OSLO WARRIOR UNDERSTANDING** (Oslo, 2024 — Joint statement by Russia, China, NATO, and Scandinavia)

Not a treaty.

Not a law.
A gentleman's agreement among militaries who understood restraint mattered more than victory.

He had helped draft it.

He read aloud:

"An enhancement must never permanently alter a soldier's biology."

He wrote this line on a yellow pad.

Short duration.
No permanent change.
Must metabolize within hours, not days.
No alteration of reproductive cells.
No cumulative damage.
No dependence.

He paused.

"These rules," he whispered, "exist because without them, enhancement becomes ownership."

He did not know Zar-Chai's chemistry.

But he knew Viktor.

And Viktor had been given this document two years earlier.

Sokolov pressed the intercom.

"Get me Viktor Baranov at Sverdlovsk-17. Immediately."

**Scene Three: Viktor Baranov's Office, Sverdlovsk-17**

The phone rang.

Viktor Baranov scowled. "No one calls here."

His assistant appeared. "Sir… it's General Sokolov."

Viktor felt the tension before he lifted the receiver. Moscow never called without reason.

"Yes, General Sokolov. What can I do for you, old friend?"

Sokolov's voice was conversational, carefully so.

"How are things at Sverdlovsk-17?"

"Excellent," Viktor replied. "Production stable. Exports on schedule."

"I'm glad to hear it," Sokolov said. "I wanted to confirm something simple. You remember the Oslo Warrior Understanding?"

Viktor swallowed. "Yes, sir. I've read it."

"Good," Sokolov replied. "That's all."

The line went dead.

Viktor stared at the receiver.

*He asked if I've read it,* Viktor thought. *Not if I'm obeying it.*

That was how Moscow cleaned its hands.

He pulled up the Oslo document on his screen.

Zar-Chai violated nearly every clause.

Not metabolized in hours.
Cumulative exposure.
Possible germ-line effects.
Tremors after long deployment cycles.

He pressed the intercom.

"Send in Dr. Petrova."

## Scene Four: Petrova Responds

Irina Petrova sat across from him, composed, eyes steady.

"Irina," Viktor said, "does Zar-Chai violate the Oslo Warrior Understanding?"

She paused.

"The Oslo Warrior Understanding is not a scientific document," she replied carefully. "And I do not receive political directives."

"So you refuse to answer?"

"I refuse to accuse you, or myself," she said evenly. "If that is unacceptable, I will resign."

Viktor studied her. She was not naïve. She knew exactly what refusal meant.

"No resignation," he said finally. "You're excused."

She stood and left without another word.

## Scene Five: Viktor Alone

Viktor moved to the window and looked out at the Ural Mountains, grey and implacable.

Russia was not ruled by laws. It was ruled by implication.

Sokolov's call.
Irina's refusal.
The embassy traffic.
The quiet tightening of language.

He understood now.

He was being positioned. Not for arrest, not for exposure, but for absorption. If Zar-Chai failed the Oslo Warrior Understanding, it would fail through him.

He smiled thinly.

"If I were a Western executive," he murmured, "I'd call this risk management."

He turned back to his desk.

"For now," Viktor said softly, "let the bear sleep."

# CHAPTER 23

## Phase II: Development (Months 3–8)

**Scene One: Development Phase Results**

Mandi and I sat on the deck of our Anacortes home, afternoon light breaking through the clouds over Padilla Bay. It was the first time in months we'd been able to sit without a clock running. Phase II had quietly concluded the week before; the teams had finished their work while we took a brief escape, more symbolic than restful, knowing the real work was already done.

The past six months had blurred into a rhythm of lab reports, late-night calls, redlined protocols, and incremental gains that only made sense in hindsight. Dozens of reports now lay stacked between us. Condensed evidence of work that had once filled whiteboards, freezers, and sleepless weeks.

Our task this evening was straightforward: confirm whether NinthWave had satisfied the requirements of Phase II and determine whether we were ready to initiate Phase III—Demonstration.

I tapped the stack. "Mandi, unless something critical slipped through, we've completed Phase II with a functional prototype ready for pre-clinical use."

She nodded. "Which means we move into Phase III of the 3D Process."

I read aloud the guidance we had drafted months earlier:

**NinthWave 3D Process — Phase III: Demonstration** Objective: Validate real-world efficacy, scale manufacturing, and achieve global regulatory readiness Duration: Months 9–12 Deliverables:

- 50 double-blind human clinical trials
- FDA / WHO documentation package
- Military and civilian deployment readiness

**Ethical Directive:** Therapies must demonstrate dual-use humanity, advancing both defense medicine and global civilian health.

I set the page down. "In plain English, we've identified the problems, solved them, and documented the risks. Let me summarize."

## 1. The Deep Burn Salve

"Cam and Nacheda-san's teams delivered exactly what we set out to build.

SW-9A penetrates beyond the epidermis and dermis and is carried, via DMSO, into the deep tissue layer where burn propagation continues after the initial injury. There, the encapsulated, DNA-bombarded SW-9A alkaloid is released.

It does not kill cells. It halts necrosis, prevents lateral damage, and triggers regenerative signaling, the Root Connection Principle-telling injured tissue where to stop dying and where to begin rebuilding.

In simple terms: it works below the surface, where the burn keeps spreading, and heals from the inside out. Nothing currently in use does that."

Mandi added, "That's the breakthrough."

## 2. Pilot Production

"Chris confirmed with James Pharmaceutical plant manager Clay Brown, that pilot-scale production is feasible using Pacific Yew aril skin. A dedicated line is already operational at the James facility outside Seattle."

She turned the page. "Now for the yield math."

## 3. Yield Math and Raw-Material Constraints

"In early trials," Mandi read, "a single one-inch aril yielded approximately 5 cm² of usable skin-equivalent material. Each three-ounce tube initially required 0.2 cm², producing roughly 25 tubes per aril.

"After six months of refinement, Cam and Nacheda-san reduced that requirement to 0.03 cm² per tube, with no loss of therapeutic effect.

"That yields approximately 166 tubes per aril—a six-fold improvement."

I nodded. "That materially changes feasibility."

"And Caleb believes," she continued, "that through controlled mineral balance, thermal cycling, and stress modulation without root disturbance, we may increase average aril size up to four-fold. If validated, that would raise yield proportionally."

"That would make him the first true yew agronomist in history," I said.

She paused before finishing.

"But the constraint remains," she said. "Arils are seasonal, but renewable. Trees take decades to mature. Yield now scales across annual harvest cycles, but remains bounded by biology, ecology, and time-to-maturity. Phase III can't ignore that, even if per-tree output improves dramatically."

I leaned back.

"So abundance isn't the problem," I said. "Time is."

## 4. The Russian Yew Question

Mandi lifted another report.

"Chris and Cam visited the Libby Montana yew grove quietly last month. The arils are naturally larger, the skins thicker, and alkaloid density higher. Morphology suggests a close cousin to the species used by Georg's Russian supplier. Genetics are not yet confirmed."

"And when NinthWave says 'not yet confirmed,'" I replied, "we pay attention."

## 5. Ready for Demonstration

I skimmed the final summary pages.

"So here's where we stand, Mandi:

- We have a functional Deep Burn Salve prototype that can reach the deep burn layer and initiate regeneration.

- We have a pilot production plan at the James taxane plant.

- We have yield math that makes Phase III feasible, even with the ecological constraints.

- We have enough raw material to produce fifty-five three-ounce tubes of active salve and fifty-five tubes of topical placebo, enough for a-fifty-patient double-blind clinical trial with a small reserve."

I set the stack down.

"In other words, Phase II has done its job. We're ready to move into Demonstration."

Mandi leaned back in her chair. "Then Monday we bring the NinthWave team onto the Quantum Whisper Bridge, lay out where we stand, and let them help shape the Phase III plan."

"And two days after that," I said, "I will go back to the Pentagon and tell the Admiral and team that we're ready to treat real burns."

Mandi smiled. "I'll call Skip and put the QWB session on his calendar."

We sat for a long moment, listening to the low sound of the water on the shore and the distant rumble of a tug in the channel.

Phase II was over. Phase III—Demonstration—had officially begun.

## Scene Two — NinthWave Summary & Naming Council

It was Monday evening, and Skip had gathered the whole NinthWave team onto the secure TNIC QWB.

Mandi opened the meeting.

"JP and I want to congratulate all of you for the roles you played in a true clinical-technology breakthrough. You have successfully completed Phases I and II. We are now entering Phase III—the Demonstration Phase. And let's be honest: if we don't succeed in Phase III, then the entire Deep Burn Project fails. Not just for NinthWave, but for the warriors and civilians who will be wounded in modern conflicts."

She let that sink in.

"From the status reports we've reviewed, it's clear you are ready for the demonstration. Unless we encounter an unforeseen issue, we see no obstacles to producing the clinical-trial materials.

We asked Chris and Clay to produce six-ounce tubes rather than the standard three-ounce size. JP and I made that decision for safety. Missile burns are large-area burns; these aren't the small injuries you treat with conventional ointments. We may also, for some reason, have to expand the study, and we want to make sure we have enough material."

I followed up.

"We all know we're caught between a rock and a hard place with raw-material availability. Pacific Yew yield is limited. Caleb, Danny, Chris, and Clay have been trying everything they can think of to reduce aril-skin requirements. It's a huge challenge, and we may not solve it before clinical trials. But what we do have will save lives. No one else has anything like this."

Mandi nodded and continued.

"With that in mind, we're putting up on the screen a short summary of where we stand at the end of Phase II. JP and I would like each of you to read these paragraphs and approve them as the factual summary of our status."

I projected the Phase II Summary onto the TNIC wall.

Fifteen minutes passed. There were a few minor edits, then unanimous approval.

Mandi looked around the virtual table.

"Now," she said with a rare smile, "for the fun part. Up to now we've used the generic compound name—SW-9A. It's time for the salve to have a Brand Name."

I added, "We've narrowed the criteria. Because of raw-material limits, this will not be a broad consumer product. This is a controlled-use, deep-burn regenerative therapy. The name must reflect regeneration, burn specificity, and its lineage to SW-9A."

Skip unmuted.

"We fed your criteria into TNIC and grouped the possible names into the two categories."

The screen lit with the two columns:

**Category A — Scientific Controlled-Use** (Names that sound clinical, secure, and mission-ready)

**Category B — Narrative / Human-Oriented** (Names that evoke meaning but are less suitable for classified deployment)

Mandi gestured toward the screen.

"We think the name should come from Category A. Clinical, scientific, unmistakable. Let's talk through them."

That's when I stood and wrote three words on the digital board:

**REGEN — BURN — 9A**

Silence fell across the TNIC Bridge. A silence that meant recognition.

Caleb spoke first. "That is exactly what the compound does. Regeneration and burn healing. And the 9A keeps its scientific truth."

Cam leaned forward. "And it ties directly to the alkaloid lineage. Perfect."

Skip nodded. "RB-9A is excellent for secure communications. Short. Clear. No confusion."

Mandi smiled. "Let's say it plainly."

She turned to the team.

**"RegenBurn-9A. The world's first deep-burn regenerative salve."**

Chris exhaled softly. "That's it."

One by one, heads nodded across the screens—Vienna, Japan, Montana, Mammoth Lakes, Anacortes.

I pressed SAVE on the TNIC interface.

"RegenBurn-9A is official," I said quietly. "I'll present it to the Admiral on Wednesday."

Mandi closed the meeting. "We'll finalize the Phase III plan next, but tonight NinthWave has named something extraordinary."

The screens blinked out one by one.

RegenBurn-9A was born.

**Scene Three — The Pentagon**

The group of four gathered in Admiral Brewer's office conference room. I had just finished my status report on Phase II.

"Admiral, we finished Phase II by giving our new compound a Brand Name: **RegenBurn-9A**. We thought we should emphasize the regenerative process of the formula."

The room was silent for a few moments as the team considered the name. They were also, as usual, waiting for the senior person in the room to speak first.

"I like it," Admiral Brewer said. "It's simple, and we can shorten it to **RB-9A** for our usage."

Both Hank and Emily agreed.

I picked up the conversation again. "I'd now like to summarize Phase III and ask for your approval to proceed."

Admiral Brewer nodded. "JP, you and your NinthWave team have done an outstanding job. You are on schedule, and best of all, you have created a clinical breakthrough that will benefit our troop rotation and the well-being of our warriors. I also want to add that, after we solve the raw-material issues, all civilian populations both friendly and enemy, will ultimately benefit.

"With all the forecasted results we must not forget, we still have a long way to go to prove that what we have discovered will really do the clinical healing we have forecasted. I am encouraged that you have the material to make the product necessary for the clinical trials.

"I will be interested to hear from you Emily, on how you are going to accomplish the clinical trials. Specifically where you will get the patients, where they will be carried out, and how you will keep the trials secure. First, JP, provide us with the Phase III plan."

"Aye, aye, Admiral." I put up a slide with only a few words.

**PHASE III PLAN**
- Produce final product tubes for the double-blind clinical study
- Assist in the clinical studies and adjust as required
- Continue studies to increase yields
- Develop production plans along with the Pentagon's planned first-level distribution quantities

"Admiral, Phase III is straightforward. It completes the NinthWave Deep Burn Project and is scheduled to run for the next two months.

I feel confident that we will be able to complete our responsibilities within that time.

"Without losing confidence in our Pentagon teammates, we respectfully request that there be some flexibility in this final Phase to allow for delays, corrections, and other unplanned events. What we have done together in ten months will make a great clinical development case study for the *Harvard Business Review*. We have been fortunate enough to be ahead of schedule up to this point. But Phase III is where we move from theory to delivery. Admiral, within the Pentagon contract negotiations, is there such an amendment?"

"JP, I hear what you are saying. I am basing my answer on the fact that you have more than delivered on Phases I and II. To tell the truth, you, NinthWave, and the people around this table have performed admirably. I also realize, JP, that up to this point in the project you have had primary control. In Phase III you will be relinquishing some of that control to clinical and distribution operations.

"I will add an amendment to our contract as follows."

The Admiral had anticipated my request; this was not the first time a contractor and the Pentagon had reached a shared-responsibility situation. He read from a legally approved amendment.

"The Pentagon recognizes that a shared-responsibility situation will exist in Phase III of the Deep Burn Project. In order to meet the Pentagon's requirements for delivery of the final product, the Pentagon authorizes the Contractor to continue with the project with minimal delay. Compensation will be negotiated based on facts following the successful completion of the project. Funding will continue without interruption through to an authenticated conclusion of the Contract."

"Do you agree to the amendment, JP?"

"Affirmative, Admiral."

"Fine, JP. Now to the approval of your plan: it is approved, and funding will be released for Phase III."

"Thank you, sir."

"Emily, it is your turn to provide us with your clinical trial plans," the Admiral requested.

"Thank you, Admiral."

Emily opened a folder labeled *RegenBurn-9A Clinicals.*

"Admiral, I've been evaluating options for the human trials for more than a month. My clinical team and I concluded that traditional U.S.-based trial designs simply cannot meet the parameters of this project.

"So before I present the plan, JP and I would like to request one adjustment."

She looked directly at Admiral Brewer.

"Sir, the original contract specifies a one-hundred-patient clinical trial. That number is theoretically ideal, but practically impossible under our constraints. We recommend a fifty-patient trial; twenty-five treated with RegenBurn-9A and twenty-five receiving the placebo control. This will still yield statistically valid results and keep the operation secure.

"Our reasons are threefold:

1. **Raw-material constraints** — Pacific Yew aril skin remains scarce; we cannot responsibly produce RB-9A for one hundred patients without jeopardizing Phase III supply.

2. **Timeline compression** — two months is not enough time to ethically locate and enroll one hundred deep-burn candidates.

3. **Operational security** — this is a classified, controlled-use therapy; smaller cohorts reduce both exposure and detection risk.

"For these reasons, Admiral, JP and I request formal approval to reduce the clinical trial cohort to fifty."

Emily paused. Brewer took a slow drink from his mug before answering.

"You have my approval. Frankly, I always felt one hundred was aggressive for a field burn study under secrecy. Proceed with fifty."

Emily nodded once, relieved.

"Thank you, Admiral. With that established, I'll brief you on our clinical structure and the site we've selected for the trial."

She glanced down at her notes.

"This plan uses the assets of my institution—the University of Texas, Houston Burn and Reconstruction Center, where I hold my primary research appointment. I am also a joint affiliate at Memorial Hermann's John S. Dunn Burn Center, the largest burn unit in Texas.

"We propose to conduct the clinical trials using my hospital's providers in our privately supported burn clinic in Reynosa, Tamaulipas, Mexico, about a five-hour drive from Houston. I helped the hospital establish that clinic. I discussed this option with NinthWave, and they agreed to the plan.

"I feel that the Reynosa area is uniquely suited to the trials. Reynosa sees a high volume of severe burn trauma—from refinery accidents, industrial fires, home explosions, and cartel-related civilian injuries. This offers a population of deep-burn cases ethically, quickly, and without raising unnecessary flags.

"These trials will not constitute formal FDA approval for U.S. marketing, that's not our objective at this stage. What we will do is set up a dedicated ward in the clinic that meets FDA-grade clinical-trial standards.

"We will ask NinthWave to prepare two sets of visually identical six-ounce tubes:
- One containing RegenBurn-9A;
- One containing a control formulation identical up to the deep-penetration stage, but with Neosporin as the active ingredient.

"To preserve blinding and security, Neosporin will be purchased over-the-counter from multiple pharmacies. Only the trial's chief medical officer will know which patients are being treated with and without RB-9A.

"The challenge will be the patients themselves. The non-RB-9A group will likely experience more breakthrough pain, whereas the RB-9A patients may not. To offset this difference, we will assume a baseline analgesic effect from Neosporin in the control group and adjust our pain-scale analysis accordingly. Our goal is to measure the incremental pain reduction and healing benefit attributable to RB-9A.

"We will preferentially enroll patients with burns on extremities, arms or legs, so we can keep systemic effects as neutral as possible. Systemic versus non-systemic impact will be monitored through standard vital signs: temperature, blood pressure, heart rate, and lab markers.

"Patients will be identified only by code. The Department of Defense, NinthWave, and my institution will be the only entities with access to the code key.

"As for the Mexican government, our hospital has very strong relations with federal health authorities because of our longstanding charity work in Mexico. NinthWave can establish, with the Mexican oversight committee, a separate, clearly defined study area within the clinic to supervise the trials."

Hank leaned forward.

"Admiral, there has been a recent joint Mexican–U.S. program that will likely increase the number of deep-burn candidates for Emily's clinical trial.

"In their ongoing fight against drug traffickers, the two governments have just signed an agreement called Follow the Money. Jointly, they are tracing where drug-trade dollars end up—cartels, shell companies, families, transportation networks, precursor suppliers. The objective is to intercept the money flow and either divert or stop it, depending on the situation.

"The Mexican government believes that once the Money Flow program gains momentum, they will move to targeted missile strikes against cartel compounds. They do not want what happened to parts of Venezuela to happen to them. That will inevitably produce burn casualties, not specifically warriors, but real patients with deep, complex burns.

"These patients will come to Emily's clinic. They will not be experimental subjects; they will be burn victims in need of care. But they will give us proof of compound concept and outcome."

He added, "For your information, the closest town to Reynosa with significant cartel activity is Río Bravo. If I had to guess, Admiral, Río Bravo will be on the early target list."

"Well," Admiral Brewer replied, "we seem to be getting ourselves into armed combat whether we like it or not. But I expected nothing less when we started looking for military-grade cure protocols.

"Speaking of military health Hank, do you have an update on the Zar-Chai troop enhancements the Russians are giving their soldiers?"

"Not much, Admiral," Hank said. "Our intelligence lines on that subject have gone quiet. We still believe, based on Emily's analysis, that there is a long-range issue with troops drinking Zar-Chai. But at the moment, as far as we can tell, the Russians think we are interested in troop enhancement, not burn care.

"U.S. intelligence is keeping this exposure in its back pocket, for a more advantageous time to bring a Geneva and Oslo-Agreement violation case against the Kremlin. For now, we are watching and listening."

Hank cleared his throat. "There's one more piece of intelligence you should have before you go to Reynosa."

Both Emily and I looked up.

"The cartel compound in Río Bravo isn't just cartel," Hank said. "It's a mixed-operation site. DEA and DIA have confirmed that at least one of the factions funds its fentanyl and meth labs with technical 'advisors', that's the polite word, from Russia and, more recently, North Korea."

Emily frowned. "Military?"

"Former military," Hank said. "But in both cases, 'former' usually means 'still on someone's payroll.' We've seen men with Spetsnaz gait mechanics and DPRK medical tattoos. The working theory is that Russia launders small-unit personnel through cartel operations for hard-cash funding and live-fire experience."

He paused.

"And there's another layer. Some of the Russian-linked personnel appear to be consuming the same stimulant tea compound. The one Emily identified in her early toxicology review."

That got the Admiral's attention.

"So the tea has already moved outside Russia," Brewer said.

"Possibly," Hank replied. "Or Russia is using the cartel site to test whether the compound works on non-Russian physiology. We don't have proof yet. But if missile strikes hit Río Bravo, and they will, there's a chance you'll see Russian or Korean combatants among the burn casualties."

I felt the weight of that. Emily did too.

Hank continued, "If you see any unusual physiologic patterns—rigidity, tremor, temperature instability, I want you to flag it. Quietly. Facial recognition and biometrics will handle the rest."

Admiral Brewer nodded.

"Good catch, Hank. That reinforces why this trial must stay covert."

"Thank you Hank. I think that is a good place to end this meeting. Congratulations to all for the great job you are doing for the health of our Military, You have exceeded my expectations.

Blocks away the Russian US Embassy sleeper filed his report: 'Admiral Brewer, met with previous noted team. Subject matter still a mystery.' The report made its way up the Russian chain of command to Viktor's boss General Sokolov in the Kremlin's U.S. Observation Activity Directorate office

# CHAPTER 24

# The Oslo Line Begins to Fracture

**Scene One: Kremlin — The Telex That Shouldn't Matter**

Corporal Yuri Krylov sat alone in the narrow telex room deep beneath the Kremlin, the air heavy with machine oil and old wiring. The Americans hadn't sent many intel lately, nothing worth reading, certainly nothing worth forwarding.

But today the printer chattered out a long strip of encrypted pulse code that made him straighten in his chair.

He decoded it slowly. Then read it twice.

**U.S.–Russian Embassy Report Update**
Emily Vargas delayed after work by embassy staff as directed.
Briefcase seized by embassy-controlled assets. Contents scanned, imaged, destroyed.
All papers consistent with burn-salve research.
No references to Zar-Chai, enhancements, or soldier conditioning.

Meeting again today: Admiral Albert Brewer, Dr. Jean Paul Kornig, General Hank McKenna, Dr. Emily Vargas. Subject remains unknown.

Analysts conclude U.S. interest appears limited to burn treatment, not troop enhancement. Continue observation.

Yuri exhaled softly.

"The Embassy agents are missing something," he said under his breath.

But Kremlin protocol was simple: anything involving Kornig, Brewer, or Vargas went up the chain.

He rerouted the message to Corporal Anya Morozova for dispatch to General Aleksei Sokolov, Director of the U.S. Observation Activity Directorate.

As the pneumatic canister snapped shut and shot upward, Yuri whispered, "Your turn, classmate."

## Scene Two: Kremlin — General Aleksei Sokolov's Office

General Aleksei Sokolov sat with his elbows on his desk, blinds half-closed against a gray Moscow noon.

He read the telex once. Then again.

"Kornig again. Brewer again. And the woman, the burn specialist." A pause. "But no enhancement. No Zar-Chai."

He leaned back and opened a thin folder: the Oslo Warrior Understanding, signed by Russia, China, NATO, and the Scandinavian Bloc. Not a treaty, but a boundary line. A rule set for what must never follow a war.

He read the articles aloud, a doctrine learned until it no longer needed thought:

Enhancements must be temporary.
No permanent change.
Must metabolize in hours, not days.
No alteration of reproductive cells.
No cumulative organ damage.
No dependency.

## He set the file down.

"If Viktor's Zar-Chai violates this," he said quietly, "I will have a problem. And Viktor will have a disaster."

He pressed the intercom.

"Morozova."

"Yes, General."

"Get Viktor Baranov on the phone. Now."

**Scene Three: Sverdlovsk-17 — Viktor's Office**

The phone rang.

Seeing the Kremlin prefix, Viktor Baranov glared at it as if Sokolov himself had pointed a finger through the receiver.

His assistant appeared in the doorway. "Comrade Baranov, General Sokolov is on the line."

Viktor muttered a curse. He had hoped the questions about Zar-Chai had died from neglect.

He picked up. "Yes, General. To what do I owe this honor?" Tone smooth. Voice tight.

Sokolov's voice was clinical, almost bored.

"Have you reviewed the Oslo Warrior Understanding recently?"

Viktor stiffened. "Yes, General. Of course."

Silence. Weighted. Calculated.

"Good," Sokolov said. "We will speak again."

The line went dead.

Viktor sat motionless. A bead of sweat slid down his spine.

*He knows. Or suspects. Or wants deniability.*

He turned toward the window overlooking the Ural foothills.

"To hell with this," he muttered. Then spoke loudly, "Get me Dr. Irina Petrova. At once."

## Scene Four: Sverdlovsk-17 — Dr. Irina Petrova

Dr. Irina Petrova entered Viktor's office quietly and stood at attention.

Viktor wasn't sitting; he was pacing.

He stopped abruptly. "Irina. Does Zar-Chai violate the Oslo Warrior Understanding?"

She blinked once. Then again.

Her answer was precise, surgical, and moral.

"I do not wish to respond to that question, Comrade Baranov."

Viktor stared at her, anger rising.

"You know what our product is being used for."

Still standing, she folded her hands.

"You asked me to extract an alkaloid and develop a powder for tea. That is what I have done."

"Irina," he said, lowering his voice. "Tell me the truth."

Her reply was professional survival, carefully framed:

"If our product violates the Oslo Warrior Understanding, then you will say so. If it does not, then you will say so. My work is medical science. Politics is yours."

Viktor felt something he hadn't felt in years: fear.

"Do you resign?" he whispered.

Irina shook her head. "Not yet, because science still matters."

Without waiting for dismissal, she turned and left.

Viktor collapsed into his chair.

"I am being positioned," he whispered. "Someone will be blamed. And that someone is me."

He stared at the Urals.

"Let the bear stay asleep," he murmured. "But if it wakes… it will eat the closest man."

## Scene Five: North Korea — Volunteers to the Russian Army

One week later at Pyongyang Military Hospital, North Korean military physician Dr. Choi Sun-ho typed an encrypted message to the Moscow liaison office:

To Russian Command:
We have observed unexpected symptoms in eight soldiers who returned from volunteer service with the Russian Army. All consumed the daily stimulant compound Zar-Chai provided to both Russian and North Korean troops.

Clinical Findings:
Early Stage:
— episodic tremor
 — temperature instability
 — unexplained fatigue after exertion

Advanced Stage:
 — memory gaps
— muscle rigidity
— hematologic abnormalities

Request Immediate Clarification:
— expected physiological side effects
 — gonadal hormone disruption
 — long-term toxicity data
 — safety for reproductive integrity

If satisfactory response not received within ten days, we will withdraw all personnel from the Russian Federation.

Captain Choi Sun-ho DPRK Medical Corps

The Russian duty officer read the transmission, frowned, and silently forwarded it to General Sokolov.

Minutes later, Sokolov wrote a single word in the margin:

"Viktor."

Then circled it. Twice.

**Scene Six: Kremlin — The Directive**

General Sokolov drafted a terse order on Kremlin letterhead:

To: Baranov, V. — Director, Sverdlovsk-17
You will prepare a full briefing on the short- and long-term effects of Zar-Chai. Include:
— metabolic pathway
— testosterone impact
 — two-year toxicity
 — epigenetic transmission
 — cross-population comparison (Russia / DPRK)

Deliver in person.
One-week deadline.

General Aleksei Sokolov
Director, U.S. Observation Activity Directorate

As he sealed the envelope, Sokolov murmured,

"The Americans work on healing. We have cultivated ruin."

He closed the file.

"Time to learn how deep this disaster goes."

# CHAPTER 25

# Regenburn-9A Clinical Trials

**Scene One — After the Pentagon**

After the Pentagon meeting, Emily and I both knew the clinical trials were now the center of gravity for the entire Deep Burn Project. The next two months would decide everything—the coordination between Emily's teams in Houston and Mexico, the work NinthWave still had to complete, and the precision required to keep the operation quiet.

Over coffee with Hank in the Pentagon cafeteria, we confirmed the plan: I would accompany Emily to Reynosa for the clinical trials.

First, we would fly to Houston and brief a small, need-to-know leadership group at the John S. Dunn Burn Center on the proposed trials. Then we would continue on to the clinic near Reynosa, Mexico for a walkthrough and final planning.

On the way to the airport, I called Mandi.

"Let the team know we've officially lowered the trial size to fifty patients," I said. "Twenty-five on RegenBurn-9A and twenty-five control. Chris will be relieved. Tell him to adjust the raw-material allocation accordingly."

Mandi agreed and reminded me correctly, that even fifty was a stretch given Pacific Yew constraints.

The Dunn briefing pushed close to the edge of our security protocol, so Emily and I were careful. We didn't mention the Pentagon or the Deep Burn Project by name. We described NinthWave's work as a new topical burn therapy with improved pain control and possible regenerative effects.

Explaining why the trial would run in Mexico took patience: patient availability, speed, cross-border clinical cooperation, and the hospital's long-standing charity work in Reynosa. In the end, trust won out.

A few hours later, we were standing outside Dunn, waiting for the vehicle south.

**Scene Two — The Reynosa Drive**

Emily had arranged hospital transport. An older Suburban rolled up— sun-faded paint, steel wheels, no chrome. It looked like a municipal service truck.

Perfect.

Inside, the disguise vanished. Reinforced doors. Heavy tint. A widened rear bench converted into a work couch. Power, encrypted comm ports, and a secured tablet station built into the panels.

Emily slid in beside me.

"The hospital calls this their cross-border asset vehicle," she said. "Legal hates the name. It stuck anyway."

The driver turned south.

We needed the road time. This trial had to be designed out loud—no screens, no notes, nothing to steal, just disciplined conversation.

Emily opened her folder.

"JP, let's start with inclusion criteria."

**Scene Three — Emily's Clinical Protocol**

"We need burns deep enough to reach dermal and sub-dermal layers," she said, "but not so extensive that systemic instability becomes the variable. Arms and legs give us that balance."

She read:

**Patient Inclusion Criteria — RegenBurn-9A Trial**
- Adults ages 20–40
- Both sexes, balanced distribution
- Deep partial-thickness or full-thickness burns of arms or legs only
- Burn size between 7% and 15% Total Body Surface Area (TBSA)
- Injury less than 24 hours old (time of injury documented)
- No inhalation injury
- No prior treatment beyond irrigation and first aid
- Baseline vitals within acceptable ranges

"We'll avoid torso burns," she said. "Too much variability."

"Agreed."

She turned a page.

"Because of skin-pigment variation, we'll use calibrated reflectance photometry. Healing will be measured against standardized color and reflectance references."

"Otherwise," I said, "someone will claim the healing is just harder to see."

"Exactly."

She slid a hand-drawn layout across the table.

**Ward A — Acute Trauma Unit** Neutral intake. Stabilization, fluids, debridement, pain control. No trial assignment here. This is the control ward.

**Ward B — Reconstructive Observation Unit** Mixed housing for RegenBurn-9A and control patients. Bed assignment by coded rotation. Only the Chief Medical Officer knows group allocation.

"That preserves the blind part of the trial," she said.

"And pain management?"

"Identical baseline analgesic protocols for all patients," Emily replied. "Managed by a separate protocol team not involved in outcome scoring."

"And the control salve?"

"Same base vehicle. Same feel. Topical antibiotic ointment for infection prevention. It soothes, but it doesn't penetrate."

"Good."

"Every dressing change is photographed," she continued. "Standard angle, lighting, and scale. Images upload to Dunn's encrypted server the same shift, then wipe locally. Mirrored to TNIC."

The highway shimmered.

"This will work," Emily said quietly.

"If the clinic holds," I replied.

## Scene Four - Clínica de Reconstrucción San Telmo

Reynosa rose slowly from the heat. The Suburban turned down a quiet side street and stopped behind a steel gate.

"There," Emily said. "San Telmo Clinic."

The building sat low and reinforced—white concrete, shaded walkways, a central courtyard.

"Seismic-stabilized," I said.

"Dunn insisted," she replied.

Dr. Roberto Ibarra met us at the door.

"Scientific and confidential," he said. "A good combination."

The clinical trial Ward B was clean, efficient, and ready. Ten beds. Central monitoring. The injuries would come from refineries, propane accidents, gas leaks, and sometimes cartel arson or improvised accelerants.

Ward A was larger, divided into sub-bays with strong, even light. This was the control ward.

At the far end of each Ward was an isolation room for special injury cases.

"Hopefully unnecessary," Ibarra said.

Clinical trail data room. Shielded walls. Fiber isolation. Wall safe.

"QWB feeder node," Emily said.

Outside, two municipal officers sat in the shade. Cameras watched the gate.

"If strikes begin," Emily said, "Ward A will fill fast."

"It will hold," I said. "It was built to."

# CHAPTER 26

# Regenburn-9A: Trial by Fire

**Scene One — Reynosa, Tamaulipas, Mexico**

The Mexican authorization had been signed before dawn.

Months of escalating cartel violence—armored convoys, drone attacks on police stations, refinery seizures, and mass kidnappings, had pushed the Mexican government beyond containment. Intelligence identified fortified cartel command-and-production sites operating outside civilian centers, shielded by terrain, bribery, and fear. The order was narrow and explicit: precision air strikes on verified cartel leadership and logistics nodes, coordinated with humanitarian response protocols.

There was no announcement.
No speech.
Just the Mexico President's signature, and the consequences that would follow.

**Clínica de Reconstrucción San Telmo - Reynosa**

Emily and I had just finished the clinic walkthrough when her phone vibrated an encrypted Dunn channel. She stepped aside to read it, posture shifting into that forward-lean tension clinicians get when preparation turns into inevitability.

She handed me the phone.

Operations initiated.
Mexican Air Force executing precision strikes.

Expect burn casualties.

I gave it back.
"So it begins."

Dr. Roberto Ibarra had already sensed it. The clinic had gone quiet in a way that only happens before impact.

"It will not take long," he said. "The fires will come first. The people after."

He was precise. Controlled.

"Civilian wards remain under my control. Your clinical study wards stay sealed. If you see qualifying cases, notify the administrative nurse. Once transferred, they are yours."

Emily nodded once. "Understood."

We separated. Dr. Ibarra toward the civilian intake wings, Emily and I toward the secured NinthWave clinical study corridor.

## The First Wave — Civilian Chaos

The first siren shattered the quiet.

Then another.

Within minutes, police trucks were driving through the Clinic courtyard gate. Beds started to fill with burned men, women, and children, most from the Reynosa refinery zone. Officers shouted. Families cried. Nurses ran between wards and central supply. The air filled with the smell of scorched fabric, burned skin, antiseptic.

"¡Fuego en la zona industrial'hay niños también!" *(Fire in the industrial zone—there are children too!)*

The Civilian Ward filled immediately:
A shopkeeper with blistered burns from shoulder to elbow.
A teenage boy with deep burns across both calves.
A woman pulled from a burning shed, forearm raw and shining.

Dr. Ibarra moved like a machine built for this moment.

"Airway first. Fluids. Cool—not ice."

Stretchers lined the halls. Supplies vanished as fast as they arrived. The clinic groaned, but held.

Only one civilian met our criteria: a refinery worker with patchy, full-thickness burns banded around his right arm. He was transferred quietly into the NinthWave intake bay and logged as a trial candidate.

Outside, Reynosa burned.

## Río Bravo - The Strike

The second missile hit southeast of the city.

Río Bravo.

The Río Bravo had been disguised as an agricultural processing facility. It wasn't agriculture. It was a cartel manufacturing site'reaction vats, solvent drums, improvised distillation towers producing additive drug products destined for the U.S.

The missile blast ruptured storage tanks. Solvents atomized into flame. Secondary explosions followed as scrap metal yards ignited and illegal refining pits flashed like open furnaces.

Fire ran along drainage channels. Burning foam clung to skin. The air itself seemed to combust.

Workers ran until their bodies failed them. Others fell where they stood, burning alive. Those still able tried to smother flames with coats, water, dirt. Mostly failing.

Within minutes, the road from Río Bravo toward Reynosa filled with vehicles carrying the wounded trucks, vans, motorcycles. Some moving under their own power, others pushed.

**The Second Wave — Clinical Impact**

The sound reached us next.

Deeper.
Heavier.
Rolling in from the southeast.

Emily stopped mid-step.

"That wasn't industrial."

"No," I said. "That was ordnance."

Patients poured into the clinic, this time different. Burn patterns deeper. Flash exposure. Chemical residue. The difference was audible before it was visible.

The screaming told us everything.

Two men stood out immediately, not by injury alone, but by posture. Even burned, even stripped of clothing, what remained unburned was creased. Disciplined. Military.

As their clothes were cut away, laminated military identification surfaced—one Russian, one North Korean.

Foreign "volunteers."

They were each moved directly into a secured Ninth Wave clinical room at the end off the wards; one isolation room per ward, identical layout, identical equipment, separated by thirty feet of corridor.

Assignment followed emergency triage doctrine under mass-casualty conditions; no informed consent was possible, and no blinding was employed.

*Divergence*

The different sounds coming from each of the special isolation rooms emerged within the hour.

From Ward A Isolation Room One came screaming, hoarse, and relentless. The sound of a trained man losing a battle he could not understand. Vitals climbed. Burn margins crept outward. Tissue dulled toward gray.

Control.

From Ward B Isolation Room Two came almost no sounds.

The man lay still. Breathing slowed. Muscles unclenched. When he spoke, it was calm, confused more than afraid.

RegenBurn-9A.

Emily stood with me between the observation windows of the two rooms.

"Same injury pattern."

"Yes."

"Same analgesia."

"Yes."

"Different outcome."

"Yes."

Outside, Reynosa burned.

Inside, medicine crossed a line.

**Intrusion**

A black sedan pulled into the clinic courtyard just before dusk.

Two men stepped out. Well dressed. Unhurried.

Inside, the receptionist recognized them instantly. Cartel security. The rule was simple: be polite, become invisible.

One of the men smiled.

"Good afternoon. We're here on behalf of the Río Bravo facility. Two of our people were transferred here. We are responsible for closing their files."

Her hands trembled. She pointed down the right-hand corridor.

"Thank you," the man said pleasantly. "Have a nice day."

They walked down the hall.

Every step echoed.

A nurse flattened against the wall. A clipboard clattered to the floor.

At the clinical double doors, they met Emily and me.

"We're looking for two executive workers that were injured" the taller man said. "Management is concerned."

"Our wards are full," I said, lifting my coffee cup. "We wouldn't know…"

"We don't have time to review every patient," the second man interrupted gently. "The men we're looking for will understand why we're here."

Silence.

"They're in isolation," I said. "One in each room at the end of the Wards."

"Thank you," he replied. "That saves time."

They walked on.

Inside each of the isolation rooms, came one muted pop.

Minutes later, the men passed us again on their way out.

"Appreciate your cooperation," the taller man said. "Good evening."

They left.

### Aftermath

When we entered the rooms, both men were dead. Single shots to the head.

Emily and I sat back down, hands steady only because they had to be.

"What now?" she asked.

"We document," I said. "Then we look closer."

### Autopsy — The Truth

Morning light.

Dr. Ibarra made the incision.

A hardened device lay embedded near the clavicle.

A tracker. Military-grade.

Emily closed her eyes.

"Those men weren't here to just kill two soldiers," she said.

"No," I replied. "They were here to erase evidence."

She spoke again without looking at the bodies.

"I've only seen this symptom pattern once before."

"Where?"

"In Zar-Chai field reports. Intelligence briefings. Not hospitals."

"The tea suppresses fear, delays shock, masks thermal damage," she continued. "It turns burn tolerance into a tactical variable."

I understood.

"If RegenBurn-9A counteracts that…"

"It neutralizes a weapon," she said.

### Disposition

"What should we do with the bodies?" Emily asked.

"I know it isn't humane," I said, "but if we don't take responsibility ourselves, we lose control of the situation." I paused, listening to the sounds of the ward beyond the door. "If you agree, we document everything first."

She nodded.

By morning, the clinic had reached its breaking point.

Bodies lay in temporary holding—victims of fire, smoke, collapse. Some identified. Many not.

We photographed and documented everything concerning the two men: burn margins, tissue response, residual salve effects, extraction sites where the trackers had been removed. No faces. No identifiers. Just data. Enough to remember. Enough to never forget.

Their charts were marked the same way dozens of others already were.

Unknown.
Unclaimed.

Dr. Ibarra did not ask questions. He glanced at the forms, nodded once, and signed where the page indicated transfer to municipal handling.

By noon, the bodies were gone'absorbed into the same system now carrying away victims from Río Bravo, the refinery, the industrial yards.

No flags.
No records that would survive the week.
No trail leading back to the clinic, the trial, or the salve.

The data remained.

The men did not.

Inside, the world had shifted.

## Scene Two — TNIC Confirms the Origin

## Secure Clinic Data Room — Next Day

We documented the initial clinical responses of the fifty-two patients enrolled. Twenty-six per group to offset loss or corruption of data, resulting in twenty-five validated cases in each group.

All images and samples were encrypted through Dunn's system and pushed through three-layer authentication to TNIC.

Seconds later, Skip appeared live on the QWB feed.

"JP, concerning the soldiers, the device is Russian-manufactured," he said. "Short-range locator. Heat-triggered activation. Biometric status included. When the casing melts, it transmits a dropout signal interpreted as death."

Emily exhaled slowly. "Then both commands already know they are dead."

I sent a secure message to Mandi.

Missile strike confirmed. Clinicals underway. RegenBurn-9A performing extremely well. Complication: two foreign military burn cases—one Russian, one DPRK. Hank engaged.

Her response came quickly.

Are you safe? What do you need?

Safe. Reinforced construction. I helped design clinics like this years ago. How are yields?

She replied:

Cam and Chris visited the Libby Grove. Alkaloid profile matches Russian Yew. Likely shared ancestral seed line. Caleb increasing aril circumference. Purdue Agriculture analyzing root-mat behavior. Q'ARIUM integrated data from additional Pacific Northwest groves 40–60% natural aril surface variation. Yield projections improving.

"Excellent," I typed. "Back to work."

**Scene Three — Moscow and Pyongyang Find Out**

*Parallel — Kremlin & DPRK Military Command*

Neither Russia nor North Korea knew the other had embedded observers in the Río Bravo cartel operations. Neither knew the other had implanted trackers.

But both devices activated in the heat of the explosion.

The signals did not reach Moscow or Pyongyang directly. They reached relay stations:

- Russian military signals unit inside the Havana Embassy
- DPRK intelligence cell near Santiago, Chile

Both relayed the same alert:

Operative wounded. Beacon triggered, death. Location: Río Bravo / Reynosa border district. Possible hospital intake.

For General Aleksei Sokolov, this was catastrophic.

If a Russian soldier was examined, clinicians could identify:
- Zar-Chai toxicity
- Hematologic fragmentation
- Gonadal hormone disruption
- Slow metabolic clearance
- Neuromuscular rigidity

Every one a violation of the Oslo Warrior Understanding.

If the Americans documented this, even privately, Russia would lose something no strategy could replace: moral leverage.

Sokolov convened an emergency midnight meeting.

"Authorize extraction," he said. "Quietly."

Orders followed: retrieve operatives, eliminate evidence, prevent interrogation.

In Pyongyang, the response was harsher.

"If Western doctors examine our man," the DPRK Chief of Staff said, "the shame will be ours, not Russia's."

Parallel orders went out.

Two allies now moved in concert. Not from loyalty, but fear.

They did not know that the situation had taken care of itself.

## Scene Four — Early Clinical Results

By Day 14, the data spoke clearly.

### RegenBurn-9A Group (26 patients)
- Re-epithelialization: 47–52% by Day 10
- Infection rate: 3%
- Pain reduction rapid; near zero by Day 5
- Early mobility restored

### Control Group (26 patients):
- Re-epithelialization: 18–22%
- Infection rate: 31%
- Persistent pain spikes
- High contracture risk

### Post-Mortem Findings (Russian & DPRK soldiers):
- Lymphocyte suppression
- Peripheral nerve micro fractures
- Gonadal hormone disruption
- Chronic alkaloid exposure consistent with Zar-Chai ingestion >18 months

Recovered evidence was transferred under Dunn chain-of-custody to TNIC.

Emily's nurse remained at the clinic to complete protocol uploads.

Emily and I packed our bags.

Somewhere above us, intelligence networks were fully awake.

And in the Kremlin, Viktor Baranov's last days of freedom had quietly begun.

# CHAPTER 27

# The Viktor Reckoning

**Scene One — Sokolov's Plan**

General Aleksei Sokolov sat alone in his Kremlin office, the winter light thin and metallic through the reinforced window. His tea had gone cold. His pen hovered above the single sheet of paper on his desk. The only safe place left in Moscow to plan anything without surveillance.

The tracker signal had died.

Both foreign operatives, the Russian and the North Korean, were presumed dead. Which meant the Oslo violation was contained. For now.

Sokolov exhaled sharply. "Who knows we have violated the agreement?" he said to the empty room.

His field units. Battalion medics. The DPRK command. And Viktor. Especially Viktor.

He pressed the pen to the page and began writing a multi-column plan. It was not elegant, but it was complete. Each item designed to be executed swiftly and quietly, without triggering the Kremlin's instinctive urge to form a committee.

He murmured as he worked down the list:
1. Stop distribution of Zar-Chai. Reason: manufacturing quality issue.
2. Stop production. Immediate cancellation of Viktor's contract.
3. Shut down Sverdlovsk-17. Two-month "renovation."
4. Destroy all medical records. Only Irina knows the full picture.

5.  Identify replacement enhancer. Use the candidate Viktor displaced.

He paused, pen suspended.

"Irina," he whispered. "Only Irina can help me fix this."

He dialed her number. "Irina, are you well?"

She answered with concern. "I've seen strange activity around Sverdlovsk-17. Is something happening with Zar-Chai?"

"No," he lied automatically. Then caught himself. "Perhaps. Best we talk in person. Come to Moscow tonight."

A long pause. "Very well," she said. "Dinner?"

"Dinner," Sokolov agreed. "Instructions will follow."

He hung up. He finished writing and began the implementation of the 5 plan items until Irina would arrive for dinner. When it was time to join Irina, he folded the page twice, and slipped it into his coat pocket. Leaving his office, he whispered the truth he could not write down:

"Everything begins with Irina."

He exited the Kremlin through a service corridor and took a civilian taxi. No escort, no motorcade, and headed toward the Gavrilovsky Vaults, the only restaurant in Moscow where a man of his rank could speak without being heard.

**Scene Two — Irina's Visit to Moscow**

Irina Petrova arrived in Moscow under a veil of winter dusk. From Sverdlovsk-17 to Koltsovo's restricted runway, onto the Ministry of Defense jet to Vnukovo-2, then a silent sedan to the Gavrilovsky Vaults Restaurant. The route took less than four hours.

The Vaults felt older than the Kremlin itself. She walked down the stairs through arched ceilings carved from dark stone, alcoves worn smooth by generations of shoulders and whispered decisions, iron lamps flickering with amber light. The walls bore photographs and etchings layered through centuries: Imperial officers in polished boots, factory directors with Party pins, cosmonauts on leave.

Russia had changed its banners many times. The rooms had not.

Sokolov was already seated in a deep alcove when Irina arrived. A single candle flickered between two untouched plates of pelmeni. She slipped into the booth and sat opposite him. He tapped the stone wall with one knuckle.

"These stones survived the Tsars," he said quietly. "They survived the Revolution. Stalin. The war. The collapse." He let his hand rest against the rock. "They will survive whatever comes next. So will Russia."

Irina sat, still carrying the cold of Sverdlovsk in her coat.

"You asked me to come," she said. "Something has gone wrong?"

"Something," Sokolov said as he poured her a shot of vodka. "Yes."

He slid a folded paper halfway across the table for her to read, not to keep.

"We are dismantling Zar-Chai," he said. "Quietly. Permanently."

Irina's breath caught. For months she had labored under Viktor's shadow while he chased proximity to power. Tonight, power had chosen a different shape.

Sokolov outlined the plan in a low voice—halting distribution, canceling production, temporarily shuttering Sverdlovsk-17, erasing medical records, installing a replacement enhancer. No speeches. No justifications.

Irina clasped her hands, knuckles pale.

"General," she whispered, "this is a purge."

"It is survival," Sokolov replied.

From the back room drifted the soft tuning of a balalaika.

A moment later, a singer joined in. A man past his prime, voice roughened by years rather than drink, singing a song older than the state that now claimed it.

Эй, по приказу шли мы,
братцы, Да не спрашивал никто…
*Hey, we marched by order, brothers,*
*And no one thought to ask why…*

The melody moved forward without urgency, as if it knew where it was going and did not expect to arrive intact.

Кто вернулся — тот молчал,
Кто погиб — тому почёт…
*Those who returned stayed silent,*
*Those who died were given honor…*

The words praised obedience, but the music carried something else, an understanding passed hand to hand like contraband. Survival was never mentioned. It was assumed. It belonged to those who learned when to follow, and when to step sideways out of the line.

Sokolov refilled their glasses and ordered dinner.

The pelmeni between them had already begun to cool, steam fading into the stone air. Dark rye bread sat within reach, thick-cut, beside a small dish of smetana. A plate of zakuski followed without comment— salted herring layered with onions, pickled mushrooms, boiled potatoes cracked open with the back of a spoon.

Nothing imported. Nothing ornamental.

Sokolov glanced at the table and nodded once.

"The Vaults haven't changed since I was a cadet," he said. "Same food. Same rooms. Same order of things." He gestured faintly with his fork. "Different flags. Different slogans. But when the speeches stop, this is what remains."

Irina understood immediately. The meal was not hospitality. It was proof of how a country learned to endure shortages, winters, invasions, and its own ideas about power.

"I need a replacement enhancer," he said. "A natural successor. And I need you to help me."

Irina exhaled. In this room, beneath stone older than doctrine, she could speak freely.

"There is a replacement," she said. "The one Viktor displaced."

Sokolov's jaw tightened. "The product from Volgapharm Biologika."

"Yes. R-Metilak. Temporary metabolic stabilization. Three-hour clearance. No endocrine disruption. No reproductive impact. Minimal fatigue. It meets every requirement of the Oslo Warrior Understanding, unlike the cumulative alkaloid burden of Zar-Chai."

"And Viktor buried it."

"To protect his budget," she said, then added evenly, "And his ego. And, I assume, increase his finances."

The balalaika circled the refrain again, softer now.

Не за славой — за державой,
Мы держались до конца…
*Not for glory—but for the state,*
*We held on to the end…*

Irina did not turn toward the sound. The irony was gentle but unmistakable. The song honored those who endured, not those who obeyed perfectly. It remembered the ones who lived long enough to be forgotten.

"NATO will accept this as modernization," she said. "The tea will fade into rumor."

Sokolov raised his glass. "Za nas."

Irina clinked hers. "Za nas."

She waited. Then delivered the request she had rehearsed for months.

"When this is over, you will need oversight. A medical officer with rank and authority under direct Kremlin Directorate medical mandate. I would like that role. Colonel of Medical Enhancements. Reporting directly to you."

He did not hesitate.

"Da. Double da. It is done."

Relief softened her shoulders. The candlelight warmed the stone walls. The balalaika's melody filled the hall like an old friend. There was no romance in it. Only alignment.

They finished dinner speaking not of treason or failure, but of families, winter markets, and the odd rhythm of Russian life. The things that endured when programs ended, and names disappeared.

Outside, snow fell in pale sheets. Sokolov escorted her to her sedan.

"Colonel Petrova," he said quietly, "thank you."

And she left for the airport, while Viktor Baranov's world contracted with each passing mile.

## Scene Three — Plan Execution

Within forty-eight hours, the days had moved quickly.

Sokolov executed his plan.

Sverdlovsk-17 was shut down for "renovations," halting all production and shipments. Field generals were ordered to destroy existing tea supplies due to a "manufacturing defect," cautioned only to avoid inhaling the smoke.

Irina was formally placed in charge of medical records and instructed to "accidentally" delete historical data. She initiated R-Metilak procurement under emergency modernization authority.

Sokolov called Sergei Antonov and ordered the military to exit the cancer-drug business entirely, repurposing the plant under a civilian pharmaceutical mandate.

The Kremlin Electronic Measures Unit activated an electronic containment dome over Viktor's Ural dacha.

All plan items were completed except for two—Viktor's removal and the legal severance.

Sokolov drafted the directives and had them delivered.

Five minutes later, his phone rang.

"General Sokolov."

"Aleksei! My friend! What is happening? Are you shutting me down?"

"Comrade Baranov," Sokolov said formally, "this call is being monitored by the FSB. As we speak, a military unit is entering your facility. You will accompany them to your dacha, where you and your wife will remain under electronic containment for the rest of your lives."

"But Aleksei, we are comrades!"

"Not today not ever. You are accused of actions endangering the Russian Federation. You will remain confined. It is merciful compared to a Siberian court."

Aleksei heard a harsh knock echoing through his receiver. Viktor shouts. The clatter of the phone dropping. Then Viktor's scream as he was dragged away.

Sokolov set the phone down.

"I am sorry, Viktor," he whispered. "Your greed brought you here. Farewell."

## Scene Four — Russian Yew Strategy

Sergei Antonov, FSB-cleared acting director of Sverdlovsk-17, moved quickly. He believed the Russian Yew groves could still be saved, if aligned with Western pharmaceutical standards.

He contacted General Sokolov and laid out a proposal:

- Sell stabilized Russian Yew arils and bark to Danube Pharmaceutical company under humanitarian exemption
- Retain Russian ownership of the groves
- Adopt Western harvesting protocols
- Secure Russian jobs
- Remove all military exploitation

Sokolov approved.

Sergei placed a call to Dr. Georg Messenger in Vienna. Because the call originated from the pharmaceutical division, no Kremlin monitor flagged it.

"Dr. Messenger, this is Sergei Antonov, the acting director of Sverdlovsk-17."

"Yes, Sergei. Are you safe to speak?"

"Yes. Much is… changing. Viktor is gone. We request a neutral-site meeting with you to negotiate a supply contract for Russian Yew raw materials."

Georg paused. "That is… unusual. But go on."

"May I propose a location? The Kremlin Sub-Level B-4. It is secure."

Georg sighed softly. "Sergei… a meeting is many things, but neutral is not one of them. Still, if you assure our safety, we will attend. Our team will include Dr. Vargas and Dr. Kornig."

"I will send the necessary papers," Sergei said.

"Very well. We will see you next Wednesday."

Sergei ended the call, heart pounding.

The future of the Russian Yew, and Russia's dignity, now depended on that meeting.

# CHAPTER 28

# The Russian Yew

**Scene One — NinthWave Team Briefing (Anacortes)**

**One week after returning from Mexico**, Emily and I were exhausted in a way that went beyond sleep. We decided that Emily would join us in Anacortes for a short holiday and to brief the NinthWave team. We landed in Seattle late, picked up a rental, and drove the hundred miles north to Anacortes in silence, broken only by small observations about the Puget Sound fog, the ferry horns, the lights across the channel.

It felt good to be home.

Mandi met us at the door. She hugged Emily first, long, tight, relieved, then me. The three of us sat on the deck with wine, wrapped in blankets, talking in fragments. Emily went to the guest room early; Mandi and I to our room followed soon after.

The next evening the NinthWave boardroom felt almost festive. Skip had set up a QWB conference link, everyone logged in, and you could see the anticipation on their faces. We were down to the final month of Phase III of the Pentagon Deep Burn Project, and for once the excitement outweighed the anxiety. People spoke over one another at first—questions, updates, guesses, until I finally raised my hand.

"Everyone," I said, "welcome to what may be our final full-team meeting on the Deep Burn Project. And let me begin with this: RegenBurn-9A is a clinical success."

The room went still.

I continued. "The trial proved what your work promised. Emily and I saw it ourselves in Reynosa. RB-9A performed beyond expectations. The hardest part of the trial wasn't the science, it was seeing the placebo patients suffer while the RB-9A ward was quiet, even peaceful. Once all placebo cases were fully documented, we crossed those patients over to RB-9A to end their suffering. The transformation was immediate."

Emily stepped forward. "The isolation properties of the salve weren't visible to the patients, but the burn progression stopped instantly. Pain dropped sharply. Granulation began early. Q'ARIUM analyzed every image and vital sign. The signal is real." She gestured toward the screen. "We have a breakthrough in deep-burn care. Full stop."

Chris cleared his throat. "The good news is we can support initial Pentagon supply. The not-so-good news is the long-term constraint remains…the Pacific Yew. We've identified ten abandoned groves the cancer-drug companies left behind decades ago and we are acquiring them quietly. And thanks to what Nacheda-san and Cam discovered, we can redirect the tree's energy toward larger arils. Early testing shows a fivefold yield increase. It gives us a sustainable future."

Nods moved around the table.

Cam added, "We've proven the encapsulation and DMSO transport system scales precisely. Biology plus chemistry. One plus one equals three."

Then Georg spoke on his QWB connection, slowly, and deliberately. "There is something I must share. The Kremlin contacted me through back channels. They want a meeting regarding the Russian Yew grove. It appears they are exiting the enhancement business, voluntarily or otherwise." He paused. "They want to sell raw material to James Pharmaceuticals. And they want us…me, JP, and Dr. Vargas—to come to Moscow."

Emily straightened. "We should go. While the tea they developed wasn't part of our clinical trial, JP and I saw its effects firsthand on the

Russian and North Korean soldiers in Mexico. They are violating the Oslo Warrior Understanding. Badly."

Danny asked, "What does that have to do with RB-9A?"

"Nothing," Georg said. "Except that Russia may become a critical raw-material supplier. We need to understand what's happening."

I nodded. "We'll go. Then we'll meet Admiral Brewer in D.C. With what we now know, I see no reason we can't declare the Deep Burn Project successfully completed."

I looked around the room. "You've changed medicine. Every one of you. And as our employment agreement states, you'll remain fully paid through the next six months while Emily and I identify the next venture."

No one spoke. Just pride. A collective exhale.

That night the three of us; Mandi, Emily, and I, ate at Anthony's, walked home in the cold Anacortes air, and slept deeply. In the morning, Emily flew back to Houston to prepare for Moscow.

## Scene Two — Arrival in Moscow (Baltschug Kempinski)

We landed in Moscow just after dusk. The city was a sheet of cold light reflected off the Moskva River. The FSO escort met us at the jet bridge and guided us through diplomatic customs under pre-cleared health delegation protocols, without a word.

We were driven directly to the Hotel Baltschug Kempinski. The Kremlin visible across the river, its towers glowing red and gold in the frozen air.

The security wing sat deep within the upper floors of the hotel:

- no elevator button for the level
- biometric scan at the landing
- two silent FSO escorts at each end of the corridor
- sound-dampened walls
- unmarked doors labeled only in small Cyrillic script

This was where the Kremlin placed delegations who needed to be secure, invisible, and contained.

Inside our suite, the windows faced the Moskva River. Ice drifted along the surface. Emily stood there quietly for a moment.

"It feels like we're on the edge of something," she murmured.

She was right.

**Scene Three — Breakfast Before the Negotiation**

**Hotel Baltschug Kempinski — Restricted Wing, 7:10 AM Moscow Time**

Breakfast was arranged in the private hallway outside our rooms, FSO protocol. White linen. Silver carafes. Steaming black tea. Kasha. Rye bread. Preserved cherries.

Sergei Antonov arrived at exactly 7:15 with two FSO escorts. He looked older, strained, but relieved to see us.

"Doctors," he said with a small bow, "thank you for coming. Today can change everything."

We spoke quietly, guardedly, about nothing that mattered. We avoided mentioning Viktor. We respected the omission.

At 07:40, the lead FSO officer stepped forward.

"It is time."

Handheld scanners swept our bodies, no anomalies detected. Georg's QWB cufflinks were active and invisible.

"Please follow," the officer said.

**Scene Four — Motorcade to the Kremlin**

We descended to the underground motor bay, where three identical black Aurus Senat sedans idled.

Sedans were assigned:

Emily and I were placed in the center vehicle. Georg in the rear. Sergei in the lead.

The armored engines hummed softly. The convoy slipped through back routes, then descended into an unmarked stone tunnel lit by heavy red lamps.

The FSO officer ahead turned slightly.

"From this point, the Kremlin records no audio. Your meeting is off-register."

Which meant to the FSO officer, no record. But to Georg, we will be listening.

### Scene Five — Descent to Sub-Level B-4

At the tunnel terminus, two Zaslon officers awaited us—elite, silent, armed.

We entered a lift with no numbered floors, only Cyrillic designations:

A1
A2
A3
B1
B2
B3
B-4

The descent was long enough for pressure to build in our ears and a faint vibration passing through the floor.

The doors opened onto a basalt corridor, air faintly scented with ozone from RF dampeners.

We stopped before a heavy black steel door marked:

Секция Б-4 — Закрытая переговорная

*Section B-4 — Closed Negotiation Chamber*

Inside stood a single Karelian birch table beneath a hard overhead light.

General Aleksei Sokolov waited at the far end of the room.

On one side stood Irina Petrova—uniform crisp, new Colonel's tabs catching the light. On the other side stood Sergei Antonov.

"Doctors," Sokolov said, "Russia thanks you for coming."

The door sealed behind us.

## Scene Six — The Negotiation

The room felt half courtroom, half confessional.

Sokolov dispensed with formalities, speaking fluent English. He outlined Russia's offer: exclusive sale of stabilized Russian Yew raw material to Aretē Pharmaceuticals.

Then Emily spoke.

"There is another matter."

Silence tightened.

She described what she had observed in Reynosa; two soldiers, one Russian, one DPRK. Endocrine collapse. Hematologic fragmentation. Tremors. Heat spikes. Rigidity. This was:

Zar-Syndrome.
Zar-Chai toxicity.
A violation of the Oslo Warrior Understanding.

Sokolov, Irina, and Sergei froze.

Georg followed carefully. "We are not here to expose Russia. We are here for humanitarian stability, and a quiet partnership."

Something shifted in Sokolov. Relief, fear, resolve.

"What do you want besides what we offer?" he asked.

"Legal access to the yew grove," Georg replied. "Transparency, and confidential scientific cooperation regarding long-term toxicity. In other words, a confidential working relationship with the facility, the Colonel, and Sergei Antonov."

Irina leaned forward. "If Russia has soldiers suffering… would NinthWave help?"

I answered without hesitation. "If a path exists, we will look for it and inform you."

Sokolov closed his folder.

"Then we have an agreement."

Hands met across the table—three Westerners, three Russians.

**Scene Seven — Signing, Departure, Reflection**
Signing was swift and solemn.
Six signatures.
One agreement.
A buried scandal.
A preserved resource.

As the elevator returned to take them back to the transportation level. Before I left the room, Sokolov asked me to step aside for a moment.

"Tell your Admiral," he said to me, "that Russia remembers honor, even in quiet places."

I replied, "And tell your President that the United States remembers restraint."

Snow drifted across the private Kremlin courtyard as the FSO sedan carried us back to the Baltschug Kempinski.

Georg stared out at the frozen river.

"I've negotiated contracts all of my life," he said softly. "But today I felt like I was standing on a fault line, and the ground chose mercy."

He exhaled.

"One day, a woman will survive cancer because we walked into that basement." Georg commented

# CHAPTER 29

# Regenburn-9A

**Scene One. — The Trip Home**

The trip home was mercifully uneventful, exactly what the three of us needed. After a quiet breakfast near the diplomatic gate at Sheremetyevo airport, we said our goodbyes. Emily boarded her flight to Houston, Georg turned toward Vienna, and I walked toward the KLM Amsterdam connection that would eventually take me back to Seattle.

Once settled into my first-class pod, I finally exhaled. The cabin lights dimmed, the white noise of the engines wrapped around me, and for the first time in weeks I had space to think. Not react, not triage, not negotiate. Think.

We had delivered everything Admiral Brewer asked for:

- Ahead of schedule

- Under budget

- With clinical outcomes beyond anything imagined

- And a missile-burn survival curve cut nearly in half

RegenBurn-9A wasn't just a successful product. It was a new category of medicine.

I opened my notebook and began shaping the final stages of the Deep Burn Project. But instead of relief, a familiar weight settled across my chest; unfinished threads, future obligations, consequences that would not wait quietly.

I began a list.

**Unresolved Issues — Strategic & Contractual**
- Secure Aretē Pharmaceuticals' exclusive global manufacturing rights
- Formalize NinthWave's ownership of all core patents
- Draft the Aretē–NinthWave joint research agreement, including:
    - Aril yield optimization
    - Pacific and Russian Yew grafting protocols
    - Long-cycle growth planning
- Establish Pentagon pricing and multi-year supply tiers
- Lock in NinthWave's 2% royalty on all U.S. and international sales
- Quietly analyze Russian alkaloid archives for future relevance

I stared at the list and whispered,
"A long way from kayaking in Puget Sound."

The flight attendant leaned in.
"Something to drink, Dr. Kornig?"

"Yes. Your best vodka on the rocks. Splash of olive juice."

With the cold glass beside me, I drafted clean contract language: one version for NinthWave, one for Aretē, one for the Pentagon. For the first time since the missile strike in Río Bravo, I allowed myself to believe that:

We had a future after this.

**Scene Two— Homecoming**

My Uber ride from SeaTac dropped me at the kitchen door. Mandi met me the instant I stepped inside.

We didn't speak. Just held each other…long, quiet, grounding.

It felt like I'd been gone for years, not weeks. Mexico. Russia. The Pentagon. Phase III. Time had stretched thin.

This wasn't the embrace of newlyweds. It was two people who knew exactly what they were holding on to.

"Mandi," I murmured, "I've had a very long day. Let someone else cook. Anthony's?"

"You echoed my thoughts exactly," she said, smiling.

We drove down Cap Sante as twilight settled over the harbor. At the restaurant, new, now familiar faces greeted us, people who had quietly wondered where we'd gone. We sat by the window, watching the boats rock gently in the fading light.

No NinthWave.
No Pentagon.
No yews. No trials.

Just us.

Later, beneath a cold, glittering sky, we slipped into the hot tub and made the kind of unhurried love born of deep trust and deeper history.

"I love you," she whispered.

"I love you," I answered.

Tomorrow could wait.

## Scene Three — NinthWave Alignment

Skip pulled everyone into a QWB meeting the next morning. The moment the screens lit up, the channel erupted—updates, jokes, overlapping voices, relief made audible.

I leaned back and let it wash over me. What a team. What a year.

They had built something that would change burn therapy forever, and give victims not just survival, but dignity.

Contracts moved quickly:

- Aretē: manufacturing and global distribution

- NinthWave: patent ownership and research leadership

- Joint grafting and yield optimization

- Pentagon purchase tiers and deployment priority

Only minor edits. No surprises.

We confirmed RegenBurn-9A would remain Pentagon prescription-only until yields improved.

The only labeling will be the name: RegenBurn-9A. No release of the formula. We will use a classic trade-secret model and lock the formula in a safe with limited access until the Pentagon and NinthWave approve releasing it to an approved entity.

Pentagon orders only; civilian access much later. The date of a civilian release would also be determined by the Pentagon. Since this treatment for missile burns was also a factor in military rotation of troops, it would remain a U.S. Military secret until was a sufficient supply and released by the Pentagon for commercial use.

Before signing off, I authorized the Phase III completion bonus:

$5,000 per team member.

It was earned. Every dollar.

Mandi interrupted the celebration by saying: "Wait, we aren't finished yet. There are a number of clean up items that have to be documented and completed. It is not enough that we have developed the RegenBurn-9A and satisfied our Pentagon contract. There are a number of items that we still have to do for NinthWave to declare the completion of this Venture. One thing NinthWave is recognized for doing is completely finishing a contract not just saying the contract is completed."

"Mandi is totally right and I must say I was carried away by the moment. Mandi, go ahead with your items and assignments." I said.

"Here is a list of the three major items we have to follow up on with their individual and group assignments. Groups will determine who is the leader and inform JP and me:

1.  **Manufacture of RegenBurn-9A:** Clay, Cam and Chris will work on finalizing the formula for the production of the Pentagon RegenBurn-9A as well as the manufacturing process. This will be under James Pharmaceutical protocols of production.

2.  **Incorporation of the Russian Plant:** Georg and Cam work together to develop an international formula so the Pacific and Russian alkaloids can result in an approved cancer product when feasible.

3.  **New Yew Tree:** Cam, Danny, Chris and Caleb work together on grafting the Pacific and Russian Alkaloids into an International Yew tree that has a major reduction of the 20-year Growth Cycle.

"Thank you Mandi. I am sure there are other items that will require additional work. Please keep track of the time you put into the follow-up items as you will be paid at your project rate. Are there any questions?" I added.

"I have one JP." Georg requested. "My Vienna operation is very involved in the follow-up mainly due to picking up the Russian Facility, and the cancer product that Clay will produce for us. I would like permission to make a trip to the States next month to follow up on a number of projects. I would like to visit Seattle to talk to Clay, Chris, Caleb, and Danny on the new production plan for both the international and U.S. cancer product. On that stop I can also talk to you and Mandi. Then I would like to visit Mammoth Lakes, and TNIC. After which I would visit Seneca Ranch to catch up on Sweet Water Grass™."

I said, "We don't see any reason why you can't do anything you want to do Georg."

"It is just my Austria courtesy coming through JP." Georg replied.

"No problem, the courtesy is appreciated." Mandi replied.

"If there are no additional questions, Mandi and I would like again to show our appreciation to all of you for your hard and timely work. I am sure Admiral Brewer is very happy, and your performance will result in additional Pentagon projects." I looked over at Mandi.

Mandi added, "While you also finish the clean up project, JP and I will be investigating the marketplace for our next NinthWave Biobotanica Venture. Thank you again."

"Just one final thing we have to say in this world we now live in, this project is still under secrecy and we must continue to use the QWB security net. No exceptions." I warned.

The screens went dark, the energy lingered within the NinthWave boardroom for a second and then there was hand clapping and cheering. For just a brief time a relief of tension as the group congratulated each other and went to celebrate the successful conclusion of the major project before completing the follow-up projects.

## Scene Four — The Pentagon Blessing

Two days later, we reconvened in Washington:

Admiral Brewer
General Hank
Emily
And I

The original group.

I presented the final agreements. The meeting felt less like a briefing and more like a signing ceremony that didn't need to announce itself.

Brewer's pride was unmistakable. Hank offered a rare half-smile. Emily stood calm and steady, Reynosa still present behind her eyes.

This wasn't goodbye.

It was simply: See you again.

## Scene Five — Ten Days of Quiet Water

Two mornings later, I woke to sounds of Anacortes. Mandi and I sat in our rocking chairs, Mandi was wearing one of my old Navy sweatshirts.

"You know what we need?" she said.

"A week of sleep?"

"Close, a holiday. Just us. The Nordic Tug. The islands."

She didn't need to convince me.

Three hours later, our Nordic Tug Sweetwater eased into Padilla Bay.

The next ten days unfolded exactly as they should:

- Hiking Orcas Island

- Quiet coves and drifting afternoons

- Watching J, K and L Orca Pods

- Lunch at the Roche Harbor Hotel

- Bull Kelp christening the hull

When we returned, our legs wobbled with the familiar return to land.

My phone rang. Shana.

"JP, welcome home. A courier arrived while you were gone. From Nacheda-san in Bandai, Japan. It's on the boardroom table."

## Scene Six — Nacheda-san's Letter

The handwriting was unmistakable—precise, restrained, urgent.

I opened it.

Mandi read over my shoulder, then exhaled slowly.

"There it is," she said. "The next whisper?"

I read the letter a second time and looked out across the harbor lights.

The Deep Burn Project was complete.

But something older—quieter, and very much alive, had just called our names. Nacheda-san's letter had introduced us to a potential problem in the Japanese orthopedic market that had the real potential of being adopted in the U.S. It concerned the elderly and the elderly concerned us.

And it was why the responsibility would never truly end.

And as always…
We would answer.

# EPILOGUE

## After the Burn

Three months after the missile strikes, Emily Vargas received a call on a quiet Thursday afternoon.

A nurse from the Reynosa clinic. One of the women who had worked beside us during the chaos spoke in a voice trembling between worry and hope.

"Doctors… can you return? There is a boy…he was burned in the first attack. Local care failed, the mother walked him here. They need you!"

Emily didn't hesitate. Within hours she was crossing the bridge into Mexico, the desert wind warm on her face.

The clinic was calmer now, rebuilt in places, scarred in others. But inside Ward A, the same place where the trials had begun, a woman stood beside a stretcher, gripping the rails with both hands.

The boy lying there was no more than ten and he was crying.

His name was Luis Santiago. His right arm and chest were webbed with tight, rope-like contractures, months of untreated fascial tethering, the result of cheap salves, old dressings, and chronic pain. He had once been the star pitcher of his neighborhood baseball league. Now he could barely lift his arm without crying out.

Emily knelt beside him.

"Hola, Luis," she whispered.

He looked away, ashamed to be seen like this.

His mother spoke through tears.
"He was in the first explosion.
His father died there.
We had no money to travel.
I kept him alive with what I had.
But… he cannot lift his arm.
The doctor said he will never play again."

Emily took the boy's hand.

"Luis," she said softly, "I brought something with me."

She opened her case, a small insulated pack bearing the NinthWave seal:

## REGENBURN-9A — Clinical Lot RB9A-047

Emily explained each step. Luis didn't speak, but when the salve touched his arm he inhaled sharply, not from pain, but relief. Warmth spread beneath the dressing, the same controlled sensation Emily had seen again and again during the trials.

By evening, the tightness in his shoulder had eased.
By the next morning, he could lift his arm halfway.
By the third day, he swung it freely without guarding, without fear.

The nurses gathered as he pushed a baseball into Emily's palm.

"Throw it," he whispered.

She tossed it gently.

Luis caught it cleanly and threw the ball back to Emily as hard as he could.

The sound, the solid, unmistakable crack of leather made his mother collapse into tears. He lifted his arm higher. Then overhead.

The clinic filled with applause.

Two weeks later, a small envelope arrived in Anacortes.

Inside was a photograph: Luis, in a faded baseball uniform, standing on a dusty field with his glove held high, sunlight striking healed skin like polished bronze.

On the back, written in a careful child's hand:

*Gracias. I can pitch again.* Luis

JP set the photo on his desk beside the completed Pentagon documents, the Aretē contracts, and NinthWave's next possible venture with Bandai pharmaceuticals. He stared at the picture for a long time.

This was why the science mattered.
Not the geopolitics.
Not the negotiations.
Not the contracts.

A boy could raise his arm again.
A mother could sleep without fear.
A family could dream forward instead of backward.

RegenBurn-9A had not just saved lives.
It had given one back.

JP leaned into the fading Puget Sound light and whispered,

"On to the next miracle."

And somewhere in Mexico, a baseball cracked against a bat, answered by the laughter of a child who had outrun fire and won.